One of

Us Is

Sleeping

One of Us Is Sleeping

Josefine Klougart

Translated from the
Danish by Martin Aitken

OPEN LETTER
LITERARY TRANSLATIONS FROM THE UNIVERSITY OF ROCHESTER

Library of Congress Cataloging-in-Publication Data:

Names: Klougart, Josefine, 1985- author. | Aitken, Martin, translator.
Title: One of us is sleeping / Josefine Klougart ; translated from the Danish
    by Martin Aitken.
Other titles: Én af os sover. English
Description: First Edition. | Rochester, NY : Open Letter, 2016.
Identifiers: LCCN 2015049056 (print) | LCCN 2016000525 (ebook) |
    ISBN 9781940953373 (paperback) | ISBN 1940953375 (paperback) |
    ISBN 9781940953410 (e-book) | ISBN 1940953413 (e-book)
Subjects: LCSH: Mothers and daughters--Fiction. | Loss (Psychology)--Fiction. |
    Psychological fiction. gsafd | BISAC: FICTION / Literary. | FICTION /
    Contemporary Women. | FAMILY & RELATIONSHIPS / Love & Romance. |
    PSYCHOLOGY / Interpersonal Relations.
Classification: LCC PT8177.21.L68 E513 2016 (print) | LCC PT8177.21.L68 (ebook) |
    DDC 839.813/8--dc23
LC record available at https://lccn.loc.gov/2015049056

*This book has been translated with the assistance of the Sharjah International
Book Fair Translation Grant Fund.*

*This project is supported in part by an award from the National Endowment for the Arts
and a grant from the Danish Arts Foundation.*

       DANISH ARTS FOUNDATION

ART WORKS.
arts.gov

Printed on acid-free paper in the United States of America.

Text set in Bembo, a twentieth-century revival of a typeface originally
cut by Francesco Griffo, circa 1495.

Design by N. J. Furl

Open Letter is the University of Rochester's nonprofit, literary translation press:
Lattimore Hall 411, Box 270082, Rochester, NY 14627

www.openletterbooks.org

ONE OF
US IS
SLEEPING

THE
LIGHT
COMES
CREEPING

T HE LIGHT COMES creeping in over the plowed fields. Slabs of dark clay soil thrust up in disorder, bull calves fighting in the stalls, the thud of too much body in a space too small. And the snow, so gently it lies now, upon the ridges; upon the landscape, everything living and everything dead. A coat of cold, a deep, reassuring voice. The landscape, naked, unsentimental. Here is the feeling of missing you, though no one to miss.

A landscape of lace that is frost.

The landscape is the same, and yet the landscape is never the same. Where have I been, I ask myself. My lower lip has burst like the skin of a ripe plum. Falling on the patio, knees and the taste of iron; lying on the concrete behind the rectory, waiting for the tractor to return home with the first load; if we're not up and gone we'll be in trouble. The way they come driving; hunch-backed trailers. One afternoon we're friends enough to play; we leap among the stacked bales. Fall down in between and you'll die of starvation. Like the cat we find, but that's not until autumn. So it hadn't abandoned its litter at all.

The path leading off behind the rectory fields peters out at the boundary that cuts through the conservation area, the croplands, acreage lying fallow. So much depends on it. Order. There's always a man gathering up stones in the field; new ones appearing in per-petuum, the earth gives birth to them and the piles grow large. Here and there, bigger rocks lie waiting to be collected by the trac-tor. When the time comes. Perhaps one of the boys will do it. Or perhaps the job is too big for them. The sun goes down behind the dolmen, which is older than the pyramids. So they say. How old is that, one wonders. Brothers have no age beyond the years that divide them. My sisters and I one age; we become no older than we were.

The glacial landscape, the kettle holes, where the ice bulged and bunched up the land.

I'm not sure. It felt like I was living out of sync, in every way imaginable. I've just fallen and already I'm on my feet, brushing the dirt from my sleeves, smiling to someone passing by, or to nature. It's only when I think back on something that I gain access to all that ought to be mine. You, for example.

I have returned. Something that was lies spread out across the landscape. A carpet of needles at the foot of the trees. A cape of snow, a forest of fingers, and a sky. Antlers of the red deer, Trehøje Hill, the last ten fir trees on its slopes, hollowed to the bone by wind, forlorn. This is what we're dealing with.

Oil on troubled waters.

An odd summer dress underneath a sweater and overalls.

IT'S SNOWING AGAIN. I think: when will I be able to leave, the roads are blocked and I'm stuck here. I lean forward in the windowsill, toward the pane. The marble of the sill is cold; the winter is. An afternoon in summer I put my cheek to the same sill; my lips feel too big, my hands. I push aside a potted plant, I remember that. Climbing up into the windowsill, leaning my back against the sun and the pane. The marble is cold; even though the sun has been shining in for hours, the marble sills are cold. Sticky thighs in the heat. Body longing for winter.

Or body longing for warmth.

My hands become—how can I describe it—violet; in the winter, my feet too. A color that can remind me of something like: blue. This afternoon the snowplow went past every hour; with a weariness that had to do with something other than snow, or the absence of snow, it plowed through the village, which parted obligingly. Two lengths of white. Black asphalt shining through a thin layer of broken white. I thought: broken snow is the saddest thing I can think of. And now I think again: when will I be able to leave.

I'm saving up.

Something beautiful from which to depart, something beautiful to sacrifice. It remains nonetheless, left like a shadow, a weight in the images. What could have been. Love annulled.

Are we snowed in, I ask.

My mother is doing accounts, up to her ears in receipts. Forty-nine, she says, as if to tie an end, before looking up at me.

We stare out of the window, our eyes coming to a dead end, like railway tracks in a landscape reaching the point where the workers went home and the job has been left for some other time, tomorrow or never. A sense of nowhere to go. The railway tracks lying there pointing, making the landscape a pool—or a picture you can see.

She contemplates. I understand, that thoughts like that exist: what exactly do I want, where am I going, if I am even able; and she asks me if it's a problem. If I can't get away, if I have to stay here, is it then—a problem.

I shrug. I suppose not, I say. But both of us know it is; that it really is a problem.

Cooped up in here.

The winter shuts you in or shuts you out, that's how it feels, a sense of not being able *to get anywhere*. It's inside us both. No way forward, no way back. She wants to know if I'm having trouble finding rest here. You can't really settle. That's how she puts it. There's a pause. Neither of us breathes. Again, I shrug.

I'm fine, I say.

But it's not about finding rest. It makes no difference, rest or no.

I'm in love, I tell her finally, sitting down at the table opposite her. Her eyes dart between me and the receipts; she thinks better of it and pushes them aside.

Yes, she says.

It's making me restless, I say in a voice that sounds brittle, dry, combustible. A ray of sun captured in a glass would be enough to make it break; it could happen any time. Forcible means. Because in a way I've already seen too much. An odd sense, all of a sudden, of things being arbitrary. That it's not my dead man who's important; suddenly it's someone else, the new man, on whom my life *depends*. I think to myself: can I never just be in one place. Without that magnetism. That's what the snow does. Or that's the illness the snow cannot cover up, cannot heal; the snow as salt falling upon injured raw thoughts, raw emotions. When did it happen. The snow comes in the night, and the magnetism wells up in me, I wake up magnetic, and as a magnet: held back, restrained, the entire space between this new man and me vibrates in that way. A disconcerting tension. Movements drawn in the air, movements revealing themselves—the second before they exist: then perhaps amounting to nothing. Distress at what *might* have been—so precious.

I think: this is anything but precious.

It's foreboding, the way a house can be when you arrive at a late hour and the lights are out. Or early—and the lights are out. I think I'd rather be in an unhappy relationship with someone than this: to be without someone. Without those eyes to—well, what, exactly. Give me life. All the time to bring me into being, with just a glance. Rather come into being as a stranger, someone else, than this, not to exist at all.

I am in love with the wrong man. And I am constantly leaving someone I love. A person can come unstuck, but I didn't come home for comfort.

It's about the apples. It's that.

For you have lost everything.

Nothing is like you remember it, and everything you encounter clutters your picture of *how*. Nothing remains of the world you remember; moreover, it's impossible, it cannot ever have existed. It's something other than love, something other than an absence of love. It's the picture that arises when the two things are placed on top of each other. A blurred image in which all faces become strangely open and desolate, imbued with—well, what, exactly. Time that won't; a room that won't.

And the grief on that account.

The illusionist.

I FALL AND remain lying in the grass. Lying the way I landed. Late August, a tractor idling in the field out back. The door of the cab is wide open, abandoned, mid-sentence.

There is a lack of movement in the landscape.

As though the day in fact is night; as though the sun in fact is a rice-paper lantern suspended from the ceiling, as though someone just wants to make sure everyone is asleep. That no one is reading or talking, or interfering with each other, or looking at comics. In other words: that no unreason occurs.

But then there is nothing *but* unreason: all of a sudden unreason is the only thing there *is*.

Are you asleep, I whisper to my mother.

There's no answer. The words linger, an echo from before, my dead man's voice; are you asleep, he asks.

And I was.

Or else I was playing dead.

The knots in the ceiling planks resemble almost anything. A five-legged deer. A half-moon, dripping. Something a person doesn't forget in a hurry. An apple tree with red apples in a corner of the garden, those kinds of remains; summer in mid-winter. And still it snows.

As it has snowed all day, it continues to snow.

As though the snow wants to prove something: that the composure with which snow can fall never has to do with fatigue; the snow is not sedate, it is simply *inhuman*. Like the winter this year, *inhuman* in every respect. Marching tirelessly on, repeating itself in patterns understood by no one. The dark is paled by the brightness of snow. Every now and then a red apple falls through the dim gray into the snow, here beneath the tree's basket of a crown, black bark.

A snap as the apple strikes the membrane of hard ice formed by the change in the weather that never materialized other than as a moment's hesitation in the winter, a sudden mid-winter assault—of summer. At once the frost came whistling. Then a hard casing of ice, fifty millimeters thick, now with a coat of new snow. It's all right, I say to my sleeping mother, whispering the words in the dark, sleep now.

It can be as simple as that, too.

That you can lie quietly together and be somewhere else, alone.

Yes, says my mother, awakening with a start.

Where have you been, I ask myself, what was it you needed to finish.

Can't you sleep, she asks, turning in the bed. I think: what am I doing here, in my parents' bed. I'm far too old to lie here; and always have been.

Everything is the opposite. The snow whirling up, vanishing into a cloud that cannot be distinguished from sky. I whisper to my mother: yes, I whisper, go back to sleep. She sleeps at once, without transition, departs the room, and yet lies so completely still. For years you don't notice, but then it becomes so clear, death residing in your own mother; you see your grandmother in her, her mother in yours. And then another face still, recognizable, and yet unfamiliar. A disconcerting face, this third one.

She turns over onto her side and sleeps on.

Then turns and sleeps again.

More than once: a face, my mother's face, disappearing. And the third face that can only be my own, the only explanation: mine.

Inhumanly tall grass.

Inhuman nights. I think—I have been so spoiled. I have never wanted anything I couldn't have. Now there's only one thing I want, him, and everything I don't want I can have.

Rest and stillness.

ALL THE TIME I had the feeling there was only one thing left keeping me in this world. But then one evening we parted. And the morning after, I'm still here, alive regardless. I do not wake, for I never slept. You have gone home to Frederiksberg, where you now live. You have a room in a large apartment, and you sleep in the same T-shirt as when you slept with me. You are deceased, and yet you are there, alive and well.

Without me. There in that way.

The morning slips in with the sun, that's how I think of it; that the morning begins somewhere beyond the ice-cream kiosk and the fishermen on the far spit on the other side of Langelinie, that it enters the city, passes through Østerbro. The sky is poorly sealed, the sun thin and liquid. It pours into the streets from the bottom end, pushing cars and people in toward Rådhuspladsen, out across Amager, Islands Brygge.

I don't know what you thought you had done that evening, un-burdened your heart, I suppose, but then it was all so much heavier than before, your heart included; that's how it must be. You think something will last, and then you endure, and somehow—live with.

I imagine there to be someone, but then no one is there.

I felt sure of a mother, always, but perhaps she, too, is to be struck off.

I climb into the bed, pull the duvet over my legs and put my arm around her. Now I have returned to the landscape I thought would always be there.

Is it still snowing, my mother asks me.

I nod. Yes, it's still snowing.

Did you feed the birds.

Yes, I fed the birds.

I SIT IN a corner of the living room, yet in its midst. I can sit like this, here on the white sofa, and all the time I am somewhere else. My mother walks past again, a shadow falls across the room, it's mid-afternoon. The shadows play on the walls and everything else around. The gardens are asleep; there is unease because everything outside is shrouded in winter and cannot breathe. The snow has fallen, upon all that is alive and all that is dead; the snow makes it all the same. All that is buried suffocates and rots, or grows and expands beneath the blanket of white; a membrane becoming thinner and thinner, a skin pulled taught. The snow creaks, the vice that grips the plants, the shrubs, the tree stumps. My mother looks out the window, disturbed by a feeling of having lost contact with some part of her body, like an arm that's fallen asleep. She picks at me with her eyes, pinches me to bring me back. All the time: the sense that her daughter lives in another world. The calamity that resides in that. Being alone, or at least without.

Shut out of one's own house.

A room within the family, a room within its narrative, a former colony now suddenly *standing alone*, and yet still reverberating with narrative.

She cannot understand how I can do it; but then she doesn't really know what it is I'm doing.

She leans forward over the sofa, places a hand on my knee, retracting it almost at once, as though it were unexpectedly wet, as though it were on fire. Winter, phosphorescent and unreal, a whimper of wind. Dressed landscapes. The snow remembers every wandering, traces left that cannot be wiped away; the snow remembers; the body does. But this winter perhaps is different. This winter, the snow perpetually blown into drifts; it snowed again, and again it snowed. It's impossible to remember anything, and yet one cannot doubt that something was *left behind* beneath the snow, something that would be found again in the spring. Beneath the layers of remembered footprints, traces forgotten, yet as recollections to remain, a latent illness that may return at any time. Awkwardly in spring, awkwardly in a broken face.

I look up at my mother.

Yes, I think, this face is broken. Like if you dig with too much abandon, if you dig like a person possessed or don't know when to stop. My mother's face, my grandmother's, and now this third, strange and yet familiar, which is what else but my own. A feeling of having returned too late, of rattling a locked door and knowing your things are inside. So we share this too, this puzzle of arrival, eternally postponed arrival at something that is—well, what, exactly; *still*, perhaps.

WHEN I THINK back on the days in the summer house they seem oddly architectural. As though in recollection they share something in common with structures and exact drawings. They are not allowed to be simply days. Remembered, they become *the days when*.

The days surrounding.

These are the days before, these are the days after; they fall like thick hair on each side of a broken face: how long have you known, I ask. My mother phones; I am still in bed, only then I sit up.

I'm not breathing.

How long have I known, she repeats, buying time.

There's a feeling of sitting in the back seat and being in my parents' hands. Planetary coercion. The grubby sky that hangs above the fields. The trees stand clustered like animals in the pasture.

I've known for almost a week, she says.

I nod.

I'm sorry. She apologizes. She didn't want to get in the way of my work. She thought it best to wait. I think about what she imagines I'm working on. Do the others know, I whisper.

Are you there, she asks. I clear my throat. Do the others know, I ask. Again. I think about my sisters.

Yes, she says.

So I'm the last, I think: So they all know, I say.

I sense that she nods. I picture her biting her lip so as not to cry. I bite my own lip so as not to cry—and I cry. Aren't you upset, aren't you afraid, I whimper.

Yes, she whimpers back, yes, but I've cried and cried, I've no tears left, she lies. Maybe she thinks the distance makes me blind, makes us blind.

We've wasted so much time, I think. And the two of us, I say. We've spent so much time on . . . I come to a halt.

On what, exactly. Don't you think this puts everything into perspective, I ask her.

I'm not breathing.

Again there's no answer; there is noise and light.

Yes, she says at last, I suppose so, but I'm still just as . . . disappointed.

I wipe my nose on the duvet cover. Okay, I say.

Are you coming home soon, she asks. She's standing in the kitchen doorway, looking at the birds that keep the air moving so nature won't freeze up.

Of course I'm coming home, I answer. I'm not breathing.

The question is if the mother who is telling you she is ill in actual fact is the disease itself. If a person can survive that sort of thing: death entering the stage, a burglary in the home that is life, theft of everything you knew. When you lose your mother, not because she dies, but because she becomes death, the disease that is death.

The conversation does not end with our saying goodbye and hanging up; it's as though we simply become quieter, as though we're standing in an open field, walking backward, away from each other, speaking with increasingly greater physical distance between us, and eventually we can't hear each other anymore, we put down our phones, each on its own surface. The sound of my mother's phone on the sideboard and the sound of my own phone on the dining table.

She goes out to feed the birds. I look out across the sea. I'm not breathing. Everything is still, or there is some other music, detached from the image. It's not music, it's a sound of something unfamiliar, something you don't really know anymore.

WHEN I LIE down in my bed at night I look like a woman lying down in the grass and becoming a heap, a dead calf. I lie down and think: have I risen; I'm in doubt. All that went before. The days. The ones to come. I sleep and do not dream; I am awake in sleep and tell myself a *different* story just to find peace. I tell myself about the vegetable garden at home, my mother presenting it with a pride more usually characteristic of mountains; she tells me about the various varieties. There are four rows of potatoes: Secura, Sava, Folva, fingerlings. Half a row of them. She points them out, one by one. I remember the plan of the vegetable garden, the sheet of paper with four lines, one row of this, another of that:

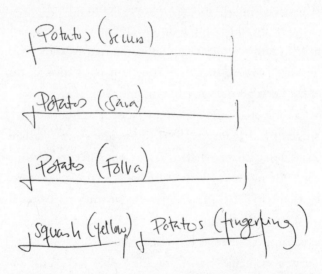

The rows of potatoes run parallel with the hawthorn hedge. On the other side runs the willow from which she was going to make baskets, only she never found the time. It became a kind of willow hedge instead. Not inferior, just something else. Another dream that never was. The fruit bushes, black currant, red currant, hanging over the path like those standing passengers on trains. Calves and trees. Disappointment. She digs up a potato plant with the spade, squats down and inserts a broad silver spoon between the small shiny tubers. The spoon is inherited and is black, its entire surface oxidized apart from the worn area on the underside of the bowl. The spoon makes the same sound as the spade—when it cuts through stony soil, washed in spirits.

YOU'RE CRYING, SAYS my dead man, concerned and reassuring all at once, sounding like someone coming home to an unexpected table, lit candles and food full of promise. I try to smile.

Am I, I say in a voice that seems cleansed of all humanity. Or the opposite, a voice that is all too human, as though too much person has been pressed into the sounds.

My attempt at a smile makes my face look atrocious.

It's evening. I haven't talked to anyone since I talked to my mother; I don't know what to say to my sisters. I'm not sure we have the same mother; I'm not sure we're a family anymore. When did it get to this, I think to myself, but maybe it was like this always. That we are neither one body, nor one family, or else: maybe a family is not the same as a *family*. It's a construct; it's like that because we can't endure anything else. We excuse ourselves, saying some plants resemble others, that some animals do; we're a bunch of flowers held together by string; an arbitrariness that steps forward when least expected; the stalks wither and the string becomes loose; when it starts to *rustle*. Thoughts rustle, a home, the faltering family. A home revealing itself to be something other than a home. Rustling. A place that is always someplace *else*, a different light there; and then the clatter of homelessness, the body that threatens to abandon thought; what remains then, one's good intentions.

And there you stand.

An idea of a home, ideas on the whole; what do we need them for. There are those we take with us, and those we don't. It can be as simple as that, too. No bus to pick you up, no bridge built to take you across. A fortuitous delay, or a delay hardly fortuitous at all; the fatality of a certain hesitation that is thought's expulsion from the body or the blood, the fact that one might never arrive. Those who came with us, and those who didn't.

THE
LANDSCAPE

E VENING WALKS DISCREETLY in and occupies the afternoon without a word; you can hear its breath. The darkness is
only aggrieved light. You have driven all the way from your parents'
house in Risskov to meet me out here. You sag at the knee like an
uncoiled spring, as if to oblige; your forward lean makes you spill
your words. I watch you greet my parents, you bend down to pass
under the low-hanging branches that drape across the paths and are
lips.

You have missed each other, I see.

Should it make me feel guilty.

I think so.

Being in the way, or something; I feel nothing. Shame, perhaps.

My mother's hands are gray. I decide to ask you later, when
we're on our own. If you noticed, if you thought about it too.

But she's alive, you'll maybe say. Or: why talk of gray hands
when she could be dead.

Her gray hands pour the tea. A couple of years ago you were not
a guest. That was then. Eight years in a family is enough to become
a fixture. Not drawing attention, and yet alien. Having a body in

a different way than indigenous family. At times you were here more than me; making yourself tea, hardly anyone noticing. No one offering to help or show you how and where. I, however, have always been a guest here. As you were a guest outside my body, homeless there. The no-man's land outside. I think you sensed it. You felt nothing else.

I ought to write about my mother.

I think: I ought to be able to write about her; write her into existence without breaking her and changing things. Simply write the book or the poem, the best possible, the most accurate picture. The way she is for me. Left to me. Like someone else, but like her, too. Whoever she may be.

But all my words—they become *something else*. The portrait of you, of my dead man, only now do I have the courage. I think you always hoped I would. Write about you, the attention. To make another person one's own, to consume them. There's something more real about the people you don't know, the ones you call strangers. The closer you get to someone, the more unreal they become.

A wish to be seen; a desire to vanish completely in someone else's eyes.

But then that's not what happens. Maybe even you're disappointed when you realize you don't stop inhabiting your own body just because you're taken over by someone else's, another's gaze, movements. To be evoked, brought forth in the eyes of another and in language, to encounter oneself there—and find another. What resembles, and what is: and something in between that appears. Somewhere else entirely. Unsparing. The drawing in the hand; holding up a pencil, one eye shut. Measuring you, measuring one's mother. Scientifically almost, yet ending up the opposite.

My images mingle unpredictably with life.

I leave nothing untouched, and still there is the constant, alarming sense of something emerging somewhere between reality and what is conceived—something that is not without history, but newborn. Moreover: the world moves, you move as I watch. Without touch, without hands.

And thus I may be compared to natural disasters.

You sit on the edge of the sofa. Run your hands repeatedly through your hair and laugh. You have a beautiful face, I think to myself. I haven't seen it for some time. I haven't seen it for a long time, and yet it has changed. It's hard to say in what way. Or to put a finger on it. But it's like it's drawn. The way fatigue accentuates a face, deepening the lines, darkening the lips, the lips beneath the eyes; the jaw and chin in need of a shave. You look up at me: it's so good to be here, you say.

I nod.

The days now.

An odd passage between something that was and something perhaps, perhaps not, to come. There are days where you think: when love reveals itself to be something else, life too will reveal itself to be the exact opposite. It's a transition, a time existing between two states: something that was, and something else to come, but a time at present that wants no gender.

I live here with my parents now, I tell myself out loud. He nods. That's good, he says. But you've got the apartment in Copenhagen, when you come back.

I sit quite still, hearing my mother explain it's just for a bit: why not stay here for the time being, so as not to be alone. Being alone is no good, she lies.

I stare.

There's no sense in being alone, best to stay here, at home, for a while.

Yes, I say: now that I've been deserted and think I'm going to die. They laugh, and I smile. The days are impossible. Not being home, not being away. Trying to live somewhere, a place, to find a way back. The uncertainty that grips him now—so dismal, a reminder that nothing is ever the way you leave it. That time actually messes things about while you're gone. The purple beech dying, elm sickness, the Eternit roofing; plastic bags lifted up by the wind and settling in the hedgerow by the slope; the electric fencing falling down because the wire broke, and nothing can keep the rotten poles upright anymore; now the snow has come, now everything's in boots of snow, the trees have drifts at their ankles, houses clutching the land, snow clambering up the houses. Above the clouds is a sky that cannot be seen. A few cracks one afternoon, but then they too are clawed back. An unfamiliar car pulling in, then pulling away around the bend. A longhaired cat from down in Vrinners, however long it might survive, *up here.*

My father is resting on the sofa opposite. He lifts his foot and wriggles his toes in my mother's face. She laughs. I wonder where it comes from, her laughter. There would be several possibilities, I think to myself. She shoves his foot away: no thanks, keep your smelly feet to yourself. And you; the laughter inside you can only be from one place, for you have so few chambers, none superfluous: a chamber for what is fatal, another for, what should we call it, the feeling when things can be that simple, that pleasing. It sounds so easy, just two chambers, the fear and the joy, and yet it's so impossible to deal with. I keep mistaking the two signatures, mixing them up all the time.

Only then I don't mistake them at all.

Death and love; death and sickness and the anesthetic in one compartment, love in the other. And then all the time love comes creeping in across the fields, in sentences like: take care.

There's something heart-wrenching about people when they possess consciousness, at least, their eyes full of it—eyes that grow fat upon the clearness of the thought: that there is nothing else, and guess who comes out on top.

Amputees.

It's like there's not enough protection.

Take care, I can whisper.

And you know what it is I need you for, what you must help me postpone. You become distant again, but that's only natural. There's nothing odd about a heart without atria not working properly; anything else would be alarming. You are a construction built not to endure, but to demonstrate, without uncertainty, that this is no way to survive.

The fact that you survive nevertheless, another day, another day.

IF I SURVIVE you, I told myself, you will become a monument. If I don't, the monument will be me.

IN THE VILLAGE where I grew up, the houses weep in the mornings. Smoke that cannot be told apart from fog rises in columns from the rooftops. Sagging structures, lopsided farm buildings long since abandoned, gutters drooping like tired eyelids.

Cycling past the houses one morning in September. Hearing an early apple, a scabby Ingrid Marie, drop onto a heavy lawn, hollow earth. The will to remain standing, a feeling of *I want this*.

My dead man's utterly impossible infatuation must be exposed as impossible.

And the houses are upright today, upright tomorrow. The village will not be moved, not for anything.

Farm buildings endure. The farmhouses themselves.

There is a strength inside those who inhabit such dismal places; the need to *preserve*. In the storm they draught-proof their windows and tie down tarps.

Of the two of us, one is forever in doubt.

I WAKE UP. The room is no longer cold, but the bed is clammy and damp. It keeps hold of its dankness. The room faces out back and is used only when we girls are home, seldom now.

My younger sister is always busy, we all are.

A rush and bustle handed down through generations. Sit down here awhile. Work unfinished. The cold of the sheets and admonishment. I don't really know what it is to feel welcome. I know what it is to belong. Except then I become unsure.

I feel, though with a delay.

Always ahead.

I meet you and immediately I see everything. A pair of scissors catching just right on a length of cloth, the blade finding its direction through the texture that is the fabric's skeleton; the cloth opens and is a fruit whose flesh is white. Such moments I live for, though never discover until later. Like when you sit there thinking it's too late, now, to think of whether to stay a second longer.

What if you stayed too long.

What if you stayed forever and never went farther away than that you could responsibly allow yourself to take a taxi home.

When such things happen, thoughts that arrive too late, they consume you and refuse to let go of your pale body, my pale body—trembling with something like doubt. I know nothing, and yet I have seen everything. The realization that resides in that; that there are eyes that *see*, and eyes that do not *know*.

A wish to be recognized as the person you are, to find such eyes, a human gaze.

Cross-eyed days in which you hope. Most days are like that, most eyes.

I am tired and wish to see clearly, a gaze that is knives and scissors, an incision into what really is. That's how I want to see, and how I want to be seen. It'll be a mess, a filthy mess. Disorder everywhere, disappointment as far as the eye can see. But you. And me, who sees you. Maybe it's more than enough, maybe it's all you can ask for.

THE APPLE TREE stands in a corner of the garden, this winter, and already back when. I have been with my parents a couple of days. The snow rumbled in soundlessly. Upholstered everything in frost, storm brigades of white, consuming landscapes, swallowing

everything, augmenting itself, stripping what lay in its path. Winter everywhere, a feeling of all this is mine. I wake up in my old
room. I know every knot in the pinewood, my own birthmarks,
and yours that I used to know. It's strange how the body's memory
will and won't by turn. Gathering blackberries in a bowl, sticky
fingers curled around the bunches of fruit, occasional berries punc-
tured, some still green, forgotten by the sun, most simply ripe; dark
pearls dropping from their stalks, into a hand that both catches
and picks, a hand that can do whatever it wants, and at the same
time: I have forgotten the feel of your body. I don't even know
what it looks like anymore. The picture won't come together. We
have become strangers to each other. There are clothes I remember
better than you. Perhaps I've never known what you looked like.
When you're standing there midstream. The smallest and largest
things a blur of *movement*. Constantly somewhere else, directions
and plans, and looking over your shoulder. All the time, *transition*.
Getting there—soon.

The way I always had this noise in my ears, something like:
you'll take care of it. And: I'd really been hoping.

Now I no longer know you. We've both forgotten most of it,
we all have. That's what we have left in common, a lot of good
forgotten. Something gets lost in the translation from then to now.
Something dilutes and becomes flaccid, something else now loud-
mouthed and staggering—homeward—toward a home that never
was, a wandering in search of a bicycle you know you left here,
someplace, somewhere around here, only it never existed, it was
a horse, perhaps, already waiting in a stable somewhere. The kind
of stable where the animals sink to the concrete floor to be extinguished by thirst, and the electric light bulbs, too, go out, one by

one. The kind of place that exists in the world, waiting for the getting there you keep putting off with all your searching.

The room is an abandoned corner inside me. That's the feeling I wake up with. And the sounds of the house are already mine, and the same. The house has a smell; it meets you head-on in the mudroom as soon as you go in; even before you begin to struggle with footwear; the sounds of the house. The rooms, swathing all movement with sounds of their own. All seven or eight rooms, swathing your thoughts.

The fact that you no longer exist for me doesn't mean that the sound of your boots, that commotion outside the door, on the stairway on Marselis Boulevard, doesn't exist. Some things remain, in the face, the body that remembers—the body that denies; the body, the least reasonable of all. A wish to barricade the body, to keep his hands away, hands everywhere; a celibacy, that wasn't about denying myself, a lack of desire for something, as you suggested, a frigidity that was most of all, perhaps, always a simple fidelity toward a man I hadn't found yet. A person I found—only then to not find at all. Restlessness in the evenings, the assault of love, restlessness in the mornings, sleep as violence. A mockery. And your eyes, the reproach, that waste of—well, what else, but a squandering of love.

I get up and it's like unfolding a worn-out sheet of paper, long forgotten in the depths of a bag, rediscovered one day by the lake while searching for the apple you know you brought with you. The sun shining coldly, early in the day or late evening. My father potters about the kitchen, making sandwiches, stirring some porridge. The gas stove squeals, the light squeals. The sense of prelude, going out. My mother's fingers poring through stacks and piles. They do not speak; the radio is on. The porridge bubbles beneath its skin, rising like a swollen lip, a finger jammed in the door, a boil fattening in the dermis; a living membrane, bursting, gasping, wheezing, and whistling. What am I doing here, I wonder, and know the answer at once. I came here for the apple tree, and because I remembered something like: we're always here for you. And in no time I've realized it's not enough.

I need to leave.

Only the apple tree keeps me behind, its branches turning to hands that clutch and grip, and I plummet: here I am.

HIS NARROW BED jars against the wall, next to the unreasonably large window. He is inside her, thrusting as if there were something there that needed dislodging. As if she and the bed are to be shoved through the window and out onto the balcony she never wanted him to buy anyway. She actually thought she had always been the sensible one; actually thought she had looked out of that window about a hundred times before.

No, she thinks now. I never did.

SHE CLIMBS THE hill, the light is the color of white cabbage; you should see me. She thinks back on a morning in Sweden when they were together there; she was wearing a straw hat. They argued about the cafés they passed, there was always something wrong.

She, limping along behind after twisting her ankle one afternoon on the rocks. Shade or sun, prices, the feel of the place: always something not right, and they would go on. The sense of time running out while one is still on one's way. An abiding state of not getting there, postponing arrival. Moving on, the mystery of destination—lack of completion, forever in motion, on our way there, on our way home, or just: somewhere else.

Direction in everything, movement toward.

Except then their patience ran out, and they sat down at a place called Selma and ordered breakfast. There was something about the way the S was drawn that reminded her of a circus. Too embellished by far, a mess of decoration. She rested her foot, keeping it elevated on a chair on which they placed their backpacks and a cushion. Her injured foot, throbbing in time to the flapping of the flaglines against the poles on the harbor. A woman was opening a little kiosk by the boats, struggling with a sign that wouldn't stay upright; it was annoying her, her movements grew more abrupt.

He poured milk into the tea, said he loved traveling in that way, without a plan. She nodded and sipped from her cup; I only ever think about *living* there, she said. What she liked about this place, this trip, was the thought of living, having a life here, studying at the university with all the ivy crawling up its walls. A solid weight of ivy. She nodded toward the buildings. To wake up and go to sleep in this place, relieve the body of all its solemnity and expectation. No more expectation; the curse of it. Joylessness. He went inside again to get some salt. The sign tilted, the woman from the kiosk had disappeared into its octagonal structure and was now making coffee. Six, seven, eight measures of ground coffee. Is she beautiful, she wondered. The sign fell over; the woman didn't notice, could hear nothing on account of the wind. One thing is what's going on inside, the work taking place there; another is what happens outside.

THE BARK OF the apple tree is black; alone in the garden, black. It cuts into the winter like calligraphy. The winter paints white dogs yellow and makes the night luminous and in a way unreal, anesthetized sleep blowing through the streets, a flood of quiet, quiet.

The tree is a shadow of another, realer world. That's what I think.

And the apples are still attached, too red, and certainly too late. Droplets suspended on black branches. They hang there today, they hang all night; not being able to see them in the dark doesn't mean they don't shine.

There is a small handful of images to which I keep returning. A hierarchy, belonging to the body and the mind, they are pictures of the emotions; they won't let go. You go back to them, again and again. Wanting to get closer. Occasionally it happens, in spite of everything, in some way or another you manage to *gain access*. A moment: to reach them and show them, return them to the world. Then, perhaps, you're able to recall. Everyone has these images; four, five or six of them. It's all about coming closer; they are what you write toward, paint toward; they are what you want to say and to share with other eyes. Another's gaze. You speak, and you point, though perhaps no one is there to see. Look, you say, perhaps. How then to hand the image on, to implant it within another, within you. That's the issue. Whether you can even carry them alone.

Whether I can; I need the eyes of another, another voice to share it with; it's too much a burden, and I write with the *expectation*.

At the top of my hierarchy is the image of the apple tree with its bright apples.

There is an image of the bedroom window with light streaming in, a morning in summer, the panes in need of cleaning; cobwebs, and some leaves from the purple beech. There is an image of a pair of espadrille sandals on a bathing jetty; the sea that stretches out behind, a sleeping body; it is autumn, and no one in sight. An image of a stable after the animals have been put out to pasture for the summer.

The catastrophes you encounter in life may seem unreal, but they are: real. The alienation that makes you think that some people are more real than others is a construct; people are no more or less alien, no more or less *real*.

More *people*, as such.

And always impending: that slap in the face, for not having known; not realizing that particular unreality was just a matter of . . .

Of what. Of eventually swallowing one's knowledge of the world—swallowing one's own ideas about knowing anything at all.

We know so very little; so little that what we think to be knowledge is hardly worth reckoning with at all; instead we ought to settle for being pleasantly surprised if, on the edge of all things, against all expectations, our assumption should be disproved.

If it turns out we know just a fragment of the world.

Constant motion, collapsing buildings and meticulous work in stone. The unfamiliar as a wall we must forever scrabble to remove in order to find our humanity there and perhaps even love someone.

Pass on one or two images, share them with someone else, a *you*. That kind of motion *into the world*. An escapism in reverse, a tower I build to be more able to see what is there.

You, for instance.

A desire to see you.

THE SNOW CAP creaks. the floors beneath me, too, feet remembering. You can trust the body. The body remembers like a hundred horses.

The apple tree is a kind of reconciliation.

I decide to go back home, but then I stay anyway. The days are like those that come after the death of a close friend. I was told the news, only then I forgot, and now I grieve, my grieving body, without any recollection of what caused the grief.

Who.

I stop and put down the wheelbarrow in front of me; who, who is it I miss. My nose is running, a dribble dissecting the oval of my face. Her father draws an oval in the air. That's your face, he says, an oval.

But her face is streaked with mucus.

The light falls in stripes.

The panes are laced with snow, movements inside her parents' house framed, embroidered. No one is dead. The wounded are legion.

THEY EAT TOGETHER, it is summer, and she has opened the windows of the apartment wide. She wants to eat in the park, but he doesn't feel like it; it's too much hassle, it's only food, he says, and she says it's only five minutes by bike. Extinguished in asphalt; the tossing heads of heifers exasperated by flies, shaking loose the brain.

There is not a breath of air inside the apartment, which smells like bottled summer; the sun vanishes behind the building opposite. The apartments are preserving jars, eyes; plums molder, voices, a partial vacuum, merely, keeping everything in place, home. They've had new balconies put in, the railings aren't there yet, children can still fall out. She stands in the afternoon sunlight, imagining catastrophes again.

Soon, dinner is the only coming together. He goes to bed when she gets up. She snuggles up beside him and falls asleep, a couple of hours before he wakes; I miss you, he lies, I miss you, he confides.

I'VE BEEN HERE before, she says.

Impossible, he says.

SHE THINKS: THE summer is nearly gone. She thinks about what she was doing while it was there, she didn't even see it, didn't see it happen. He thinks about how hectic it is—has been. They stand there, feet scuffing at the gravel of the parking area in front of her parents' house. Or: he has woken up and lies, watching her sleep. Her half-open eyes. He reaches out and extends his index and middle fingers. His arm is trembling. It is four o'clock, just before his fingertips reach her eyelids. *Don't wake, don't wake, quiet, quiet, quiet, quiet.*

She has the same effect as streams that ripple over stones, through landscapes with lakes. Fledgling birds. He draws her eyelids down with his fingers, wanting them to reach the moist edge, the horizon above the lash. He wants to shut her down for the night. Tally her up. That's what death is: unsentimental.

But they aren't children.

Have never been.

WHEN SHE'S IN that mood, she thinks of it as an insult, this sick urge to translate, in everything, bypassing art and writing. The need to *understand*. An insult, like asking Jesus to work as a circus hand, seeing him pass the paraphernalia to the magician when it's time for his bravura piece: water to wine, with the aid of only deception and berries. A circus hand.

Ta-da.

The craft of it.

What's the point. Gallows humor, greasepaint and flight: pretense, everything. And the hostages you take with you, cage in with your words, images and references, the world's eternal guessing games and sick urge to translate.

Where something comes from.

As if there were an agenda, as if it wasn't enough to be delivered to have that power. Delivered to have power over what none of us has any power over. As if, and this is what she may think, as if people even understand what it means. To have power. To possess words and speak about the world, to evoke something that is something else and yet exactly the same: a self-contained life. Whether it means anything, whether there's a difference.

But then all of a sudden it makes sense, all of a sudden that's the only thing there is: difference. That surprising leap, no matter the body, no matter the place, simply a feeling of this being: *fatal*. A span between breathing and drawing a face in charcoal. Shading the areas where the light doesn't fall. A vegetable garden, the planning of it, a face, planning that, and watching both grow from out of your hands, outgrowing you. Writing some words down on paper and hoping they keep that tension inside. A gluttony, imperceptibly becoming necessary.

She is not breathing.

So she is no longer in that spiteful mood of *emptying*. When all you do is get angry and hollow.

So maybe you can keep yourself together after all.

So maybe you can exist a bit longer, or not a second more.

That kind of leap, that kind of balancing on tall, narrow walls between city courtyards, on the dykes facing the sea, she thinks to herself, that kind. And: that's how it has to be; a real body, writing, everything else an insult, and imagining anything else as *purer than* is pretense. Thought. Whiter. Purer. More important. Choices like that don't exist: between one thing and another. She's not sure what she wants to be; and the worst part is she still hasn't the slightest doubt that she would be easier to love. That way.

Without her self.

Purer, more pure, more: woman. More person, or just more an actual person. A white, West-European man, maybe even she could be, only as a woman, of course, not quite as valuable on paper, but worth a bit more in the belt. That would be where she could hang. First on her mother's skirts, later on a man's belt, a dangling head with empty lips, red eyes; take what you want, here's person *enough*.

YOU'RE HOLDING SOMEONE'S hand, she says.

Silence then, on the other end of the phone. It's as if the room closes in on her, she can feel it, a room whose walls are wool, shrinking as it starts to rain, and the rain is boiling water.

Do you know your voice is different when you're in Sweden, she asks him.

No, I don't.

She walked late through the city, along Søndergade, Bruunsgade, past Ingerslevs Boulevard and on up to Marselis Boulevard. Semi-trucks thundering along the roads; she has the feeling she needs to lift her skirt as she crosses Marselis Boulevard. Relentless traffic, a river that can only be crossed in that way. She's been looking forward to their talk, or has thought about it, pushing it ahead of her like a heavy cart.

I miss you being here, she says, and plugs a charger into the phone. She wishes she was lying. But when she says it, it's real. And there she is, tethered to the wall, that cable.

Come back.

Come back, I need you, she says, and that too becomes real. That too is real. Like it's real that she will forget him every day, as she has already forgotten him. He is inside her, no matter how far away he travels on her money, his own; that's how it is. Can you miss something that's in the flesh. Maybe you can, she thinks. Or else it's meaningless to talk about missing or not missing, maybe it's more a question of wanting home. Whatever it is; the look in his eyes, mostly, his eyes on her, evoked in that way, in his eyes.

That's how she thinks about it.

Is that a problem, she asks herself. With all that delay, all that displacement. Out of body and back again, the look of an eye, the sewing together of two who are dead. So that the heart may nonetheless pump sufficient blood; and then again the image of a beech tree, drawing water ten meters into the air, upward into a lush green crown that cannot keep itself together and yet defies all guidelines as to what colors actually are, what you can expect for your money, your blue eyes. She is not with him yet; she is alone, walking beneath the lilacs, on the path toward the church. She sits down there and is seven years old, eight perhaps. Toes cold, as toes always are cold in churches, the way you can always find someone to grieve for. The dead, or those who survive them. The dolmen in the field, a plough edging ever closer, ten centimeters a year. Yet still it is there, and snow may fall. You think about all those years, and then that snow rumbles in, leaving the face of the landscape immaculate. A face seen for the first time. This is what snow does. On top of everything living, everything dead.

He sighs, and says: I'm tired.

She nods, and stares out the window. In the building opposite, the lights are turned off in two different apartments simultaneously. It's like the building is given a face. As if a face can ever be symmetrical. She has a tooth missing on the left side of her jaw; it never came out, all that appeared was an angular gap. Her nostrils, too, are different. A conception of symmetry where there is none; an eye, drooping; your eye, drooping as you drink. Terrible, crooked faces: all there is.

She exhales against the pane, as if the night could be expelled, as if the night could be extinguished.

Are you there.

Yes, she answers. I'm still here.

Do you miss Agri, her mother asks her one day; she is seven years old and they are on holiday. Captured on film. You see the child's face change: yes, she says, her face a moon of pale bread. On someone's tongue, a wafer dissolving, someone else's body, someone else's notion of homesickness slowly absorbing into the body.

Yes, she said.

What do you miss about Agri, the woman with the camera asks.

The answer never really comes. Everything, she says. By then the camera had been switched off.

THEY ARE SPLITTING the bill at the restaurant when her friend asks her who she grew up with.

No one, she says.

It hangs in the air; they laugh.

That's why, she thinks. I never grew up with anyone.

Her friend's eyes gleam with something that looks like sympathy, but is something else instead: recognition. When something

alien is no longer alien, because it is voiced, that's when you understand. The coming home in that, laid bare in the world together.

HE IS STRONG, and she wishes they were more like each other.
Something other than always the opposite—the reverse. But then:
that's not how I see it at all. They're waiting for word, her mother is
sick. There's been a long break, and she can hardly remember him.
Always these breaks, crushed pearls in between, well, other crushed
pearls, broken teeth. My dead man, she whispers. That's what she
calls him now. That's what he is, even though he's standing right
there. Picking his clothes up off the floor; they are exactly as he
left them, as if the trousers still contained his legs, as if putting on
clothes becomes more difficult by the day, having to share the space
inside them with himself, yesterday, and the day before, and the day
before that. Clothes too tight, so much body having gone before.

He doesn't hear.

She is envious of him; his strength, if only she had his strength,
dogged to the point of trembling, and always tired.

At the same time, it frightens the life out of her.

That kind of strength. Arbitrary. It's there, and then it isn't. She
thinks: it's like his strength isn't *his own*. It comes, and may leave
him, without predictability, without any rhythm besides: utterly
rampant. His strength comes with anger, it assails and consumes
him. Besides that—the X-rays show nothing. Strength as a tumor, a
shadow, with arteries and veins, issuing out into the body and leaving again, leaving him behind. Looked at in any other way, it has

nothing to do with strength at all. She just wants the same option of *staying*. Remaining in *one place*.

You always had to smoke.

I don't know.

There is a pause, and in that pause she and her two sisters are seen moving about the parking lot in front of the hospital, mechanically, in the pull of magnets stroked beneath the asphalt. They are without arms. There is a trace of cigarette smoke in the air. There is a trace of sound, drawn as waves in the air. Green and red waves, rising and falling. Her older sister, stifling her anger at seeing her sister smoke.

They share far too much history, it reaches too far back. Together and apart. He gets out of the car and takes her hand. The two other sisters keep wandering, while she has ground to a halt there, with her dead man, ground to a halt in front of the car.

It's kind of you to take us here. It's kind of you to . . . be here.

He looks at her, the way you look at something broken.

A broken face.

We share no history, I don't know you. That is what he thinks. That is what he says.

She says she doesn't understand what he means.

She wants that cohesion, the cohesion of language and what is.

But there is none. The *agreement* isn't there.

An abandoned house collapses, an abandoned tree topples in the woods, without a sound.

A broken landscape, lifeless expanses, the dead themselves, stone walls under snow. Maybe that's how it is. I'm not sure I understand what you mean, she repeats.

THE RAM LIES twitching, a pounding heart in the grass. It forced its way through the electric fencing because she forgot to give them water. The chain-link fence of before is gone, no longer cutting up the world in its steely rectangles. They sit in the tall grass at the hedgerow, and stare across the field. The sheep, the way they used to poke their heads through the metal eyes, ear tags or horns contriving to get them stuck, a head wrenching back, ear tag in the wire, the image of an ear torn in two. Now the fencing is electric, a current directed through four taut wires, a regular current, the tautness of the wires, a staff for musical notation running through the landscape here. And still the sheep strive for the grass on the other side, and still they may get stuck, become entangled.

Frightened animal eyes; the tremble of the beast, blue-tongued, mouth agape. I can hardly look.

Does she know what *harm* she has caused. Do you know what you've *done*. Can't you see.

All is silent. As yet no one has spoiled the stillness of the scene with questions. And it will never be the same. She is not breathing. It is Sunday and they are all dressed up as themselves. Their mother whips cream for the cake, there is a sense of expectation, the house has been dusted. The piano—dusted. The heaps in the living room, the piles of letters from the bank, the catalogues and receipts, the empty envelopes ripped open at the seams, all shuffled and patted together, corners aligned.

Seen through her mother's eyes: proud, upright towers of documents.

On the sideboard.

On the telephone table.

Order. Order, that is about opportunity, and a joy at what is to come. What is to come and what might come. A dizzying privilege, a naïve expectation as to what is about to happen.

But then perhaps it is anything but naïve. Perhaps it's never getting any better than this. Not so much about the joy of expectation as having trust in the world, that feeling of excitement in the stomach, leaps ahead in the mind, physically going on into the future. When the body goes on.

And then the damper on it all, that all of a sudden everything is in spite; a celebration held in spite. Harvest festival—when everyone knows it's not just bringing hard work to a pleasant conclusion, but also the start of a winter's slog. The cold. Shoulders grinding. Thoughts grinding, pulverizing more important thoughts, the disintegration of it all, feathers and dust descending like snow, or in November as rain. Descending to the feet of nature, descending upon life.

Perhaps she will not come here ever again, if she is forced to choose then I don't want to be here. They can come to my book launch, read the reviews and settle for that; or they can avoid the launch, not bother to read the book, and settle for that. Buy a postcard, or nothing. Send it, or not.

Not.

Never read even a page, but conjure it up in the imagination, unreading, unseeing.

I sit at the table, and the tall jug of hot chocolate is passed around for the second time; or else I stand out in the stable with the sheep wedged between my knees, holding a cloth to its ear. The ear has become infected and weeps. The flies can't be kept away. I bend down without loosening my grip on the animal, dip the cloth in the bucket of soapsuds. The bleating of a sheep can be this loud, an alarm that could almost dislodge the swallow's nest below the roof. Crumbling flakes of mud fall gently on my head, the image of a heart in the grass, the ram at my hand, the heart in the field. I write a letter to my mother, a last will and testament in reverse, all that is not mine, and all that is my own, something that is hers. A body I cannot possess any longer. I miss you, I write at the bottom, then cross it out again. And yet that is what I do, miss someone. It could be her, someone I know.

HE IS OUTSIDE himself the whole time. Standing now among the black-currant bushes, eating until he can eat no more. Until his eyes resemble the dark berries. She is transparent, he is a recurring dream of solidity. Someone has to touch her and think: here is a body. Here is proper flesh.

But all she does is drift.

She is the dust drifting in the stable, in every shaft of light, she is the trace of some insects in the dust that has settled, or she is out of sight upon worm-eaten rafters, the bark of weathered fence-posts, in the frost that covers the benches by the lake. She wants to be vulnerable:

give me wounds.

And then the cat's cracked paw pads, everything there is, bleeding. That, hand me that.

WE WALK THROUGH the city on our way home from the restaurant, looking in at the cafés, where the light is soft as upon the lakes. People, appearing in light, extinguished in darkness, in the depths of the rooms, up front. A thin man's cigarette dissects the darkness in two. He loiters there on the street corner, the way that can only be done on a street corner. The roads run on ahead and are home before us. I feel younger than ever before, as if I've seen everything and forgotten it all again, now finally having reached a place from which to start. Why have I never been here before, I wonder. You say the city is full of life tonight, I was thinking the exact opposite, at the moment you spoke—that the city was full of death tonight. A kind of beauty in that, in our meeting there, back to back; when you can't get any farther away from each other, you encounter each other again. I am a wall that goes right through you, and your body is distressed by how heavy it's getting.

HER MOTHER FILLS the room with her humming. She waters the plants, her hands pass over all things, invoking them—as things. It's like she wants to make herself heard above everything her daughter has done, to make sure all is not ruined. By the sadness of her being *so*. I am indebted; this is what she sees, the eyes of her older sister, she understands that she is indebted now and must repay what is owed, forever. And she must care for their mother when she gets old. Old and *bedridden*. When she no longer can feed herself.

She is malevolent decoration, that's what it feels like. Saddled with a love so mad, inhuman almost, that she can only disappoint. It's a matter of time, and then it will be so—only disappointment remaining, and a sense of having loved a child that never existed. And the reproaches will return, there will be a list:

The ram.

The cancellation, that trip to Copenhagen with her mother's sister. That never was.

The necklace.

Various items of porcelain.

The book.

How could you do such a thing.

The illness.

The illness of disappointment.

THE AFTERNOONS, SO late and always in that color, gray-red. Heat, and it was summer. Again she forgets how beautiful it is here, the stretch between Løgten and Rønde, here, where the bay is a blue belt folded into a bowl, a hand underneath the season.

A hand.

The asphalt, unsettled by the heat.

Her mother, who collects her in Aarhus or Risskov; they drive to Mols together. She picks at the fingernails of one hand with the fingernails of the other, eyes glued to the road. She is a martyr, uncertain of what she is fighting for.

So this is what she is fighting for.

They always talk on the drive home, but she has not a single recollection of any specific conversation. Nothing, but their *talking*. She recalls so little, almost nothing. A heart in the grass. A sky in the south of France, a pink sky, and in front of it a landscape in four layers: mountains behind mountains behind mountains. He in, you in, a bed one morning I return home from a long walk in the woods, you are asleep, and I stand there and am eyes, three thousand eyes.

The road is worn thin, she doesn't see it anymore. The beauty by which a person is surrounded has its own discreet ways. Only when a tree-cutting schedule or an autumn storm disturbs that order; only *then* can you see anything at all. When she can see the old man in the man she thought would give her, well—life. Life, the exact opposite of: left alone. When she can see, when I see, that the person is no good, and the life you were supposed to have together was no good—when we split up, the life that begins *there*: life after you begins here. You write to me and say the downturn ends here, but both of us know this is where *what is left* begins. The child inside its mother, the turnaround that takes place; a conversation postponing a farewell: what else. A silence, postponing what needs to be said. I am worn thin, a tree-cutting schedule, my body an autumn storm. I am old, I steal my mother's years, one after another, I steal age from the language, all the books I read make me unnaturally old, those I love make me unnaturally old; it's like we take on each other's lives, sharing it all, all the life that has been lived; and the dividing up of the estate is a mad gesture, we clutch and tear, pull the rings from the fingers of loved ones now dead, though their bodies may still be warm. We think we own, in fact, but what we own are memories, and they change all the time, are constantly getting lost. What do we want a ring for. What are we supposed to do with a finger.

We pass the lake—we go that way when possible. Through the plantation. The bends in the road that make you think you're nearly there. The light ahead, always so full of promise: here is the lake, enticing. A seduction that has nothing to do with a lie. The woods, that have nothing to do with seduction, besides this optical illusion. Expectations of things to come.

An Italian garden in spring: the rainwater channels that run through the town; a band of drought and skinny dogs, the occasional beginnings of plants that nonetheless are but dust in the sun—dry, and human.

The woods are unsettled, the asphalt likewise; in a way the heat makes no difference.

My mother starts to sing. Tentatively at first, then with gusto. There is an endeavor to make the song fit in, to be a pathway alongside the road. A sudden displacement inside me, as I sit there on the seat next to her, leaning my head against the window; a dislocation that runs from fatigue through annoyance to a sadness that mostly is about grief at not being a *big enough* person.

The trees and the asphalted roads.

The edgelands of all the places anyone is from. The woods, the borderland. Like the way she can think she is always on the periphery of her life, on her way to something better, something *else*, at least. The insects swarm, and even if you say a poppy or a daisy can break through asphalt: the trees surrender

whereas the roads do not, exactly,

surrender.

I ask my mother to be quiet, please. And we exchange glances, my mother turning her head, the car moving on through the woods at an even pace. The speed of the woods and the speed of the car and of the silence, a single movement. And her face turns into that dreadful face, transparent: a single sheet of paper, set on fire, but now extinguished. Her document face. I am not breathing.

Her head is so exhausted. Or just: *I'm so exhausted.*

It's like we keep on looking at each other the rest of the way, her mouth is open, her body breathing on her behalf, one last favor, gifts of that nature.

The woods have so many layers, you penetrate and press on ahead, trees ever darker; like when I was alone in France with the rubble, the remains of something that was no more, attempting to do something; and the layered mountains, one behind the other, so almost-infinite and increasingly bright, going against everything you ever learned. So few lights this evening, I think to myself back in time, later. Or I lock the door, am alone and will remain so, switch off my phone, for there is something I must finish. My eyes flick their way through the mountains, and I weep. The view here is nothing to write about. But it is the view here, the orange of the mountains, the various blues of the mountains, the blue-black of the mountains, letter-blue, blued letters, blueing mountains; behind the eyes behind the mountains, pitch black, pale red morning, pale red mountains, blood and blood-red and bread, the redly blueing leaves of blue mountains.

The lake, now abruptly the lake. My mother pulls in and parks. The light falls more directly here, descends; the lake is an eye in the woods. The car ticks. We sit for a while, then step out into the heat.

We swim, and our bodies decide to save us, again today. The lake is deep, its ceiling opaque; it is like the grand railway stations that were built at the end of the nineteenth century: glass and iron and light. Grass. Light. Foliage. The lake as a hall, an arrival—a feeling of here begins something else.

GRAYNESS, POURING FROM the sky.

The woods sigh, the remaining trees.

A lot has been cleared here, I tell you. And the barn over by the rectory is gone, they pulled it down.

You are quiet at the other end of the line. How sad, you say after a moment, understanding so little of what you say. I bite my lower lip to make it stop trembling like that.

You have to reconcile yourself with the thought that everything happens at a pace you cannot control. Failed love needs three months, so you've been told.

I find myself thinking you don't know what you're talking about.

But you do. You're talking about me. And dreaming I'll take three months. We both know that as it stands I've taken somewhere between eight and ten years.

You borrow something, everything you need you just borrow.

Childhood, a lover, a loan, merely; it's all a wicked party you clear up the next day, without hardly recognizing each other. Is that you. That girl you found, or the one you had found already; ten years, it cost you. Now you can feel guilty about mentioning, even thinking about me. Because *she* can't handle hearing about it. Forgetting on demand, maybe I'm eighteen again, and you're twenty-three. Subtract an entire life, and the years are gone, forgotten.

You comfort me, a pale hand smoothed over my hair, my mother's hand, smoothed along my back. She moves down into the living room to read, that night. My grief disrupts her sleep. You were breathing so erratically, she says, closing her eyes to the light of day, of evening, of night, always someone stealing her sleep.

But I am still alone in the room with your voice. We talk about antidepressants, about how they parcel up your senses and allow you not to take in the world as intensely as before.

That's just what I need, I say.

There is moisture in the air, the landscape proudly upright behind the curtains of moist air that extinguish everything. I long to return to Copenhagen, and I do not long at all. Nature is a fire blanket, it puts out something inside me. What, exactly, I can't tell. It bubbles constantly to the surface, a weeping about to erupt, a flame that is smothered beneath something heavy and tight and yet not extinguished, an ember rising in the throat, searing, burning. There are tall snow drifts on the left side of the road, on the right you can see the grass, scattered patches of green. The sheep stand with empty eyes in their railway wagon.

SHE REMEMBERS CHANGING her mind. The image was too arresting, maybe he would be frightened by her, and imagine her without skin.

She puts the phone down and feels like a traveler in shoes. In a land where shoes are unknown.

I STAND, RELUCTANT, beneath a feverish sky. Between the mountains: blood and fire, the evening sun melting onto every surface. The lake and your forehead, and my weary leather boots on the newspaper at the side of the house. Afternoon was just before, now a plunge into evening, then night. Waves, breaking. A darkness here, like a white sheet thrown into the air and straightened into place on top of furniture in the seaside hotel of autumn; absence (perhaps you already feel the absence); the way it runs amok; a sheet draped over a sculpture that is now finished, about to be unveiled. A sheet drawn out across the world; a bag pulled down over the head of *circumstances*.

I have fallen into doubt as to whether I can ever let you go. Leave you. Maybe I can.

Again, you look like you've locked yourself out and have just remembered the key on the kitchen table.

We say nothing, but walk together. Which isn't really like us at all; to simply walk and not speak. People who knew us when we were together, that summer we kept on leaving each other, would say: you talk, talked, your entire relationship into the ground. My sister said that.

You walk oddly, like your legs have become loose, like your feet have been put on wrong. At the same time, you are serious. You smooth your hair away from your face all the time. Your hair is longer, that must be it. But I know it's for my sake. As if what you do with your hand, your hand passing through your hair, is for me.

It's part of a new and better you.

Maybe that's it. It doesn't need to be complicated, we're not that sophisticated.

I stood preparing a fish, chopping leeks and carrots, the kitchen looked like a vegetable garden. You had been working on your thesis while I was at the allotment. I'd handed in my final assignment to the university, you were behind, the way you linger. The slimy trace of a snail on the asphalt, a morning in summer, later, the slime glistens in the early light; then we're back with you, being able to share such an image. The sun, scintillating in the slime. You come into the kitchen, step up behind me and start kissing my neck, my throat, I remember laughing: I'm busy, my hands are full—

Of fish, you said, cutting me off.

I mean it, I said, later. Only it never was later, only words snipping something into pieces, negotiation, in a country with no real currency. Everything is silent negotiation, in a language you don't understand. You talked too much, my sister says one evening. I wipe my nose on my sleeve. I shrugged, but the gesture could not be seen for body, a slightly shuddering body, sobbing intermittently. No, I said eventually, I don't think so.

Now I'm no longer so sure, it might be true, who knows. That, too. Language is never innocent. Conversation isn't always a good thing, time and again shared understanding is revealed to be some joint decision to let go and let the mind be lazy. Not much reaching for the sky in that.

I THINK WE'RE supposed to think back on the years we had together, and I think it's meant to be sentimental. The fields want that, the shiny dishes of windswept snow polished silver; it's like I'm thinking too clearly. I have a vivid sense of the movement that has taken place. A displacement: from love to dependence, to an expensive loan and a reward, dead or alive; and at the end of it all we walk here amid a landscape of winter: disenchanted, big ideas fallen apart. All is conclusion. Spent fireworks in the snow on New Year's Day are a conclusion. The Stone-Age dolmens scattered across the landscape are conclusions. The birds, surviving in spite. The folded sky above Aarhus Bay is a conclusion. Icicles on the fencing, conclusion. Bleeding hearts, bleeding abrasions, bleeding regret: all of it, conclusion. Blood itself, the gray-red lining inside everything living here; the people with their bodies, indoors, wild horses couldn't drag me out into that—a conclusion.

But the fact that we are walking here anyway is another matter; madness.

I SLEEP ALL through the night, a sleep that is a wading through deep snow. Knees lifted high when the mantle of ice cannot support you. Snow is new only once, then never more. You can't smooth it out and start again from the beginning. It's winter now. According to the calendar this is no crime, and yet that is exactly what it is, a crime. My joints creak, as if wrung from frozen, crystal dust about my knees. I lean out of the window and see the way the trees thrust from the ground like cold, blackened hands. The garden looks abandoned. The birds are busy stealing from one other. I think about the remarkable things that can occur. One morning you wake up without that feeling in your stomach, that sense of *emptied*, something collapsing. Perhaps you then get up, drink a cup of tea, realize it smells of something other than *back then*. And the day is no longer—insurmountable. You are no longer, not *only*, a half. You perhaps realize that you have grown. The days that had seemed so without nourishment, a frozen, sandy soil out west, empty ground; you're no longer the same, and it strikes you: you

are someone else, and bigger. It's like your person, the person residing inside your body, has grown older and younger at the same
time. More fragile and yet stronger. Certainly more attentive to
the world *that is.*

I think I am beginning to love something *that was.*

I KEEP THINKING about the red apples that nuzzle the sky.

I have an idea I might write about them. The clash of bright red
apples and a broken sky. The fact that they remain on their tree,
stubbornly, deep into winter, a time to which they do not belong,
an irregularity in the composure of the seasons. An anomaly, in
every respect.

I HAVE COME to Jutland, and you have come after me. It is Christmas, or sometime in January, you are on your way to visit family,
your excuse for stopping by.

I came on the train and arrived late. The whole house smelled of
soapsuds, of celebration, and something like hysterical expectation.
The way it smelled on the morning of a birthday.

My mother is exhausted, but alive.

This is the kind of assessment we make these days. My father is
more exhausted than alive, though fleetingly lit with joy on seeing
me. He is so proud I can only give in. The problem with families

arises immediately: a sense of annoyance, punctuated by guilt on the same account. The emotions you feel not being the same as the ones you had anticipated feeling. Anger at not simply being able to love. How hard does that have to be. To love those who are there for you, those who once more will tell you: we'll always be here for you.

The frightening suspicions you can get. The thought of having been mixed up at birth, of not properly belonging here, where I so obviously belong, the place I come running to whenever the world tightens its grip around my throat. The span between the feeling of being loved without condition and being loved on condition of all manner of things. The intangibility of that.

Just because someone is willing to die for you doesn't mean the grave lies gaping and in wait of its first opportunity. To bury one's parents is an impossibility, they are pillars before your eyes, they speak out of your mouth, and no matter how far away you remove yourself you will always be able to find your way home. Whatever that may be. A place in the world, or perhaps completely outside of it.

The fear of squandering it all and returning to nothing, an empty pit. A site of something that was. Because you turned into another, behind your family's back, behind your own.

Who is it who finds their way home in the dark, who is it I embrace in the night. Myself as a mother, later, my mother as a child I must care for, and now try to rouse as I wander through the rooms, through the city with the stroller, in early morning—wanting only sleep.

You love my family, and they've missed you. You are more at home with them than with your own parents, I think to myself.

I consider leaving you my family. Dubious donations, purchased origins, if that's even possible, if anyone can it would be you.

THE SUN CRAWLS up the walls, spring in mid-winter. Trees clamber toward a blue sky. I force the months out of my writing. They are nothing but decor and pretense.

Who knows what October will say, when it all boils down.

Who knows what November is. Tired light, tired darkness, seeping in, or not. The wetness of wet wool, I can endure. October, November, December take me nowhere.

WE GO FOR a walk, though you are not made to walk. It's not just a question of your body. It's more basic than that, a general lack of endurance. As soon as we come to the fields all you want is to turn back and go home, kick off your shoes; as soon as we see the hill of Agri Bavnehøj, that's where it starts; I sense the way your movements angle left. That veering away in you. Homeward, always in the direction of the *settled* that will not present itself. I realize there is a forbidding feeling of impaired recognition at work. We are familiar to the point of sickness. We are strangers. In love with something that was.

The houses weep in winter.

Horses cry.

The foundations are ravaged by frost, water pipes burst like blood vessels. A trickling of life, and of spring, but the damage is there, inside the mind, behind the walls.

I've forgotten my gloves. I hold my hands up in front of my mouth and blow some warmth into them; you take off your own gloves and offer them to me. You say nothing, not a word, in fact. I accept only one, putting your bare hand in mine and burying both inside the pocket of your coat. Not a word. We are like one of those watercolors folded up wet, two figures joined in the middle, drawing color from each other as we walk. We have pulse. We are. We awake in the mornings, both of us, with something on our lips, the feeling of something important that needs to be said. You and I. I try to say it, perhaps not to you. But at least, to do something.

You. I no longer know if you're even trying. If you tried. Ever.

When evening comes I am emptied, while you are more than filled, and kick off your shoes in all your fullness.

Where have you been, you'll suddenly ask.

Or else you say: You're always going somewhere, or coming back. Look at me. What's the hurry with you, what's so important it can't wait. And I'll shrug.

What *is* the hurry. But it's evening and I don't know. It has been uttered, only not to the right person, not to you, anyway.

There is a smell of something burnt, oil drums in gardens, the widower burning off cardboard and plastic. It is that time of year, that time of day. We have been out for hours. Fathers in the mudroom. The concept of mudrooms. A day in winter, an exhalation, then an inhalation, no longer than that. The day is like drinking water, there is nothing left in the mouth besides a natural order.

No thirst, simply order.

I'm tired, I say. You nod. We haven't slept enough, you add. Only my fatigue has nothing to do with sleep or no sleep. But then it's you who says: I'm tired.

THERE WAS A winter, nearly three years ago now. Three years, you say, your whole body shaking, not just your head. Such realizations come to you these days; realizations that threaten to whisk you away. You are a web—each of your corners is fastened to reality, though quite invisible. There is no reality left in your body. It's as if your conceptions of the world have taken over. Floating freely in your own web, until encountering a seam, the harsh impact of reality, the bow of a ship against the quay, vessels splitting down the middle, conceptions taking in water. This is you these days.

I still want to save you, but I know you would hate me for it, and so I refrain. I wander about myself, collecting for your charity; I will rattle if someone picks me up. But no one does; I am not the kind of a person others want to pick up. I am too heavy.

A
FUNERAL

WHEN HE LEFT her it was winter. They lay on the bed in her new apartment. Amid the city, half sleeping, winter, the kind of listless calm in which you can suddenly say anything at all without it coming as a shock.

Don't chew your lip like that, he told her. She went on reading. Stop it, he said, and slapped her hand, and then she couldn't help but look up.

Okay, she said.

There was a hum from the kitchen, the washing machine spinning sheets and dish towels and facecloths, the vibrations in their teeth. They had lived in Copenhagen six months in their separate apartments. In order not to miss out on *that*. They had left everything behind in Aarhus, that was how it felt: Copenhagen being temporary. They would be going back. They had finished university, and were ready—but for what. To fail, to be canceled.

Two of his friends helped her move. Only what you need, he said, and kissed her on the cheek, though only to make up for there being so much, that was the feeling she got. But then maybe it was a reproach. That comment, that kiss, placed on her skin like a cold mollusk, his fingers, and yet something in his eyes that genuinely relished seeing her like that: leaving something behind.

I'll take it, she had said to the landlord, and a blind fell down in the window at that very moment. She could hardly stop laughing, or else she began to cry, it's hard to say, both, probably. Things can start like that, too. When reality seems staged, that sort of timing: or when what's staged turns out to be reality. You should be careful what you write, it might turn out true. It will never be anything but.

August, and then soon after: autumn, winter; the wind gusting, her skirt a sail on the sea, the rumble of a blaze. So cold you're not sure if it's actually hot.

There were two rooms, besides the kitchen and the bathroom, which was down in the courtyard. Two rooms. She dumped a blue IKEA bag in the corner, could hear them coming up the stairs. With packing boxes. The bed. She stood still in the corner with her mouth open and her hands at her sides: so *this* is happening now. The kind of thought that occurs when suddenly you find yourself waking up somewhere else instead of where you went to sleep.

She sat in the window, got up again. Felt happy, filled with excitement. Another of those moments where you sense everything that is to come, and everything that has gone before: an unmistakable feeling of something ceasing to exist, with a beginning.

Not everything survives. Or rather, nothing does.

And then that window, stiff and vertical, hysterically opened onto the courtyard. Linden trees. In the autumn, when they are pruned back: crowns docked like tails, half-seeing eyes that blink at a sky forever turning gray. Winter, a stunted squall that will pass.

The clouds shift without pause in autumn, and she gets up from the table, sits down at the table, gets up, writes and does not write, in one seamless movement, puts the kettle on, drinks from a cup with brown concentric rings at the bottom, cuts some sprigs in the yard, they weep, the sky likewise; she forgets the water as it boils, she writes some pages, all in one seamless movement, a movement that does not belong to her.

Her feeling of guilt is a constant storm that brews inside her; a sickness waiting for a cause. A moment's fatigue, weakness, resentment. And the fever is upon her. Then she must run, she must convince her body that everything is all right, at rest, at work. Writing: she is continually in doubt as to its *validity*.

When what feels necessary isn't necessarily *valid*. Where, then, to deposit oneself but in a body deceitful.

She slept badly. It was like that.

That feeling that made her laugh when the blind fell down, when she took on the apartment; that same feeling came back to her when again she could not sleep.

The fatality of time and again believing the world is *determined* by something. Something outside of itself. Or just *determined*, in whatever way at all. Timing. Believing you can see patterns in the world is the same as imagining you can reach out of a window, hold out your hand, and wait a couple of seconds until a leaf, a feeble, tattered leaf, settles there gently, surely in your palm. The same as expecting you can fall asleep, in such a world.

And yet it happens all the time: people fall asleep. You see connections. Or you think you see connections; and for a moment you might feel you belong.

That something like a home exists.

Only it's not as simple as that; there are moments of collapse, life consists of little else.

A face brought down, revealed to be one's own.

Sensing how the sand on the beach in front of the hotel at Svinkløv is retrieved by the sea as each wave retreats. The current they warn you against, and which the body recognizes before the mind; an urge to succumb.

And that would be it.

What such an urge might mean.

She misses having a home, it's a condition.

Eventually she falls asleep and dreams about a man who says in English: *My hands are dirty, you don't want to meet me.*

The world laughing in your face like that. The writing laughs with it, that line of dialogue. It all gets entangled in the writing. What was, and what is, or perhaps may come. Sentences and lines of dialogue.

A desire to be older, revealing itself to be a desire not to lose one's childhood. Not to lose anything, whatever it might be, to maintain a hold in the flow of all things, to stand firm there and preserve. In some form, to keep hold of it all, and not leave anything behind in that burning house. Wherever you go, you leave behind you a trail of disaster, no matter what the circumstance, that's how it is. A trail of collapse, something falling outside of all recollection, all that is not remembered by anyone and is forgotten by the world. She is not quite sure, but the feeling grows stronger, she sees it in him: a kind of reverse will to live; a nostalgic reluctance toward surrendering oneself to the world that exists. That kind of panic in the tissue, a fear of forgetting. She writes so as not to forget things, or else she writes in order to forget things and invent other things more worthy of remembrance. Perhaps that's what writing is: you start moving about in the world like a sleepwalker in the night, looking for something more real, a truth there; and then all of a sudden it's sleep that you sacrifice, then suddenly the family, then everything that is valuable and means something. Dreams while awake, ideas, pulling everything with them like waves returning, returning to the sea, faces washed away, washed clean of all humanity. Or the opposite: invoking a humanity all too exaggerated: too much human in too small a space, that pealing reality when your entire being *wants* that someone else.

She thought the right thing to do was perhaps to find a life first, and only then look for a way of working that fit in with that life. That it should happen in that order, instead of carrying on the way things were; searching for a way of living that fit in with her work.

IT DOESN'T LOOK like him at all, and yet: it's him, she knows it is. As full of life as a bonfire in spring, at the beginning of March, the same look on his face, no less: confident. They visit her parents, they are still going out, they walk in the hills and she cannot forget that he tells her about a girl he used to know. Every month she ran short of money. And then, he says, when the money ran out she collected her last coins, searching coat pockets and rummaging at the bottom of bags, and then she would go to the florist's on Bruunsgade and buy flowers. Cut flowers. With the very last of her funds. How many lilies can I get for this, she would ask. How many daffodils for forty-two kroner.

He laughs, and is then silent again.

The sun beats down, she grabs at some foxtail and grass. That's what I want, she thinks. To live alone in a city, with no money, and buy cut flowers. That kind of recklessness, that's what I want.

He was too frail for this world; but it was she who was made to be the symbol; you are too frail for this world, he could say, drawing her toward him and hugging her. Or else in anger:

you're never *here*.

You're never here. Never present.

You could start to doubt which of them was never there: one of them, at least, always one of the two; somewhere else.

You're always rushing about, it's your family that put that into you, he says.

She looks up from a book. Yes, is all she says. You see, that's exactly what I mean, he says, throwing his hands in the air, his face, like his shirt, at once open and more closed than ever before.

What do you mean.

You don't hear anything, you're somewhere else.

She puts the book down in her lap. I'm here, she whispers.

We live parallel lives, he says. Every morning you're out running, we can't even wake up together, we can't even go to sleep together. We eat at different times, we live without each other.

She gives a shrug.

It's not true, she could say. But it is, true, most of it, true and yet not the whole picture by any means.

You'll run yourself into the ground like that; it's hardly surprising you're finding it hard to keep yourself together.

I'm depressed, she says. You said so yourself. You're talking about what it's like to live with someone depressive, aren't you. It's hardly surprising you're falling apart, he says. That we are.

Nothing is allowed to dry, they are a wound continually re-opened. It was always that, love is a wound. He sits down on the chair opposite, puts his bare feet on the coffee table between them.

And he was right, but it was quite as true, I think now, this winter, with the snow making everything stand out so clearly or disappear entirely; it was quite as true that you never felt the rush of being loved that I always felt. That feeling of something being important, absolutely necessary: red apples, their brightness, something lifting the day up above a simple matter of getting up or not getting up, the issue of e.g. the work ethic, something like: the doggedness of the work ethic. You always tried to convince me those things were destroying me. From within. You frightened me. But it wasn't true, I can see that now, or not *entirely*. I believed in you, even if I suppose I knew different all along.

I knew something else was true as well.

It's that too: the will of the flesh to be in motion, the work that despite everything kept me together. That gave my life the rhythm your body always lacked. A beat that enabled me to maintain a hold in the flow of all things. To press a paintbrush against the porcelain of the sink, to carefully spread its bristles between the fingers, to see the color wash away, thinner and thinner. To rinse the white sink clean, to dry the brushes. To crumple up a pile of newspaper and feel the stiffness it had gained from the acrylic paint that ran and then dried, sapless newspapers, wrinkled as old apples, a smell of fixative first discovered after having been outside and come in again. You've got paint on your cheek, you would say, and I was *in* something. You had your problems, I'm sure, clutching at you, that was when I realized; yet nothing that would prompt you out of bed in the morning, without lingering, without first wondering: *why.*

If too much time passes between waking and getting up, I suppose that can be seen as a bad sign. Too many questions, if you start asking yourself; all that time. The whole notion of having to consider in that way—a sign of desperation.

To have a matter outstanding with life or not. To be interested—at all. Some kind of undirected enthusiasm. Something like that. Or, an enthusiasm bursting out in all directions. You ask yourself the right questions, and if you still keep lying there it's because you want to, not because you don't. The difference that makes.

HE PRESENTED HIS leaving as a sort of doubt. He had kind of begun, as he put it, to see other avenues.

Other people, she said.

He let her do all the dirty work. He had never been good at consequences. Or decisions. It was as if they frightened him.

Copenhagen, in their different apartments: it had lasted six months. She counted the days. Maybe it was the kind of thing you started doing.

Eight years.

They lay on the bed in her bedroom, but she did not stay there. She got up, he sat up with his hand to his mouth, watching her, his gaze was a greased cable trapped in the door that shut, and she locked herself in the bathroom.

It was a tiny room, with no depth. She had to sit with her legs on each side of the toilet, on the floor, her head leaned against the door; banging her head back against the door in a steady rhythm that made the soap tremble like a heart on the edge of the sink.

So *this* is what you do. After eight years. After eight years, you get up from the bed and leave the room quite composed, and yet *de*composed, without form; you pass through another room, lock yourself inside a bathroom and fall apart there. A person melted, sitting in that way, stiffened, banging her head against a door. Perhaps it is the only thing that can be done. Eight years, count the days, and slowly the talk takes place, beginning with a whisper on the other side of a door. Maybe that's what it takes, maybe that's the way it starts. That kind of moment that has all of time written into it: what has been, what is to come, what never will be, and, what never was. That, too.

What's eight years.

When you're a strangled voice behind a door. That kind of thought, a counting on the fingers, counting on the teeth, on the ribs and all the body's bones. A rhythm coming through tissue, marrow and bone.

~~I MISS YOU,~~ please come back.

SHE THINKS HE'S always disappointed by the woods, by nature in general.

She comes home to their apartment on Marselis Boulevard at nine, after her kilometers along the forest paths, and he groans like timber in the bed. Pulls her toward him, or else hates her. You're cold, he says, and almost hates her there. Or else: You're cold, he says, reaching out for her wrist, pulling her down under the duvet, drawing her close; a desire to warm her from within; you're so cold, he says.

After a while she grew cunning: if we have sex now then it's done, then maybe I'll have the benefit of his guilty conscience the rest of the day. The kind of care you show an animal you've punished only to find out: there was no more water, they break through the fencing not to spite you, but because they're thirsty. She told herself she could use her body to deceive him. To deceive her own body.

For a long time she thought she had achieved the latter.

For even longer she thought she had achieved the former. But then one evening in winter she realizes she has never deceived his body at all. He has known all along, abandoning her gradually, angry at her for having allowed it. Not for her having made him do it; that's an idea you get, and maybe in some cases it's the truth, but not in this one, that's how she thought of it. He wasn't angry with her for making him do it: for being an inferior person. What he was angry about—in view of her frailty or her backbone, or both, perhaps—was that she hadn't *stopped* him. She was too fragile to accept such treatment, too strong to put up with it. Why did you put up with it.

His disappointment in her, in nature, too. Nature's pale, and in that way self-embracing, voice. It not making itself known, not

77

rousing you. Or perhaps just the fact that he had imagined something else, that it would do something else, something *more* for him, at least. That shock, of something utterly crucial.

Only it was a shock that never came, because basically you're left out all the time. Exposed in the mountains, in the indifferent care of mountains.

THE MORNING IS savage, the sunrise a mockery of art, too exaggerated by far, these new shoes that shine, and train journeys home when everything is over. The audience has gone home. All there is left is this same slow train; alternately, a dismal hotel room. Seeing him search through the kitchen cupboards for bottles that do not exist, but that *must* exist, as he says, I know they do. I know.

She lets herself in with movements meticulously emptied of sound. She pulls off her clothes, the pile she makes of them looks like a dog resting in the feverish cold of an outhouse; flat as an empty skin in the basket under the coats, crates of orange soda in the corner, crates of empty beer bottles. She can make her body look like gray porcelain, the bones of her hands may be crushed by a handshake, her lungs collapse like moldering wickerwork with any embrace.

She shoves the pile with her foot, out of harm's way, in case he wakes up and comes down before she gets the chance to do anything about it. And even then a thought occurs to her that sticks out in another direction; that her slackly dumping her clothes in that way might simply placate him, soften his annoyance, fear dressed up as annoyance or anger.

It was more like that.

An almost physical pain at waking up and seeing a new day *rise up out of the sea*, as it were, and she, coming home after running through the woods to the bathing jetty, after swimming, after, in that way having conspired with the sun, having risen up out of the sea—that was how he looked at it. That she was like vigor incarnate, as simple as that. All the serenity of her body on that account. All the things you cannot attain, only see; never have a part in, but wish for, year upon year. She bends down and messes up the pile so the various items are spread once more. An indication of her slackness, her rummaging about in the world.

Transilluminated, the rooms, on a morning like this.

You're a detector, he says, meaning: I've read what you wrote, and if you could see everything so clearly, how come you, or we, have *assembled* all that, that whole idea of how it was. How *I* was. And you, you as well.

Indeed, she thinks. Indeed, I think, I suppose loving someone is like that. Half the time you're frightened to death. The perspective. The shunting about, from seeing everything—to seeing nothing at all. That you can never go back and be met for the first time: seen. Differences outstanding, everywhere, piles of—well, what. Just piles.

THERE ARE TWO rooms.

There is him, sitting there, slowly ceasing to live; and there is her, banging her head back against a closed door. She is attempting to begin living. Later she thought it was the right thing to do. The fact that one of them had to say something, and that it could never be her.

He sits behind the door. Who knows what he feels. Perhaps he is ceasing to live. Death is there, on the other side of the door. Perhaps we see it all from above. The door between the two bodies is just a thin line someone has drawn in the picture. Later, this is what he told her, later he thought it was the biggest mistake he had ever made.

Maybe it's that simple, too.

Two rooms.

She may never have loved him more than she did that night, when she thought there was no more love left inside her. When she thought *that was that.*

And the sound of her head, banging against the door.

And the sound of flesh, rotting. And a picture of a doorstep one morning. And the picture of a breakfast table with juice. Images from an abandoned circus. There will be days like that.

THEY LIVED TOGETHER, there was hardly any skin, most of the time there was a confusion surrounding their bodies, where one stopped and the other began; one body may be switched off, the other pumps life into the unconscious body while it is unconscious. I know nothing about you, she thinks; she knew nothing about him, but maybe it wasn't true. The opposite is always a part of the picture *as well.*

Transillumination.

Love as a kind of transillumination.

Everything is very clear. Woods, with darkness falling. Looming silhouettes, all too distinct. The sky, turning completely pale at the prospect of something like night. The crowns of the trees, milking the sky with their eyes, their thoughts, stamping about the landscape, *trying*. To do what, exactly. To find a *home* there. In the midst of what is most unwilling: nature, rejecting its young, ejecting them from the nest, over the cliff. And there you stand, worming your way and trying to *blend in*.

For years she thought she had succeeded in doing just that.

And not for his sake. To become *a part*. To belong in a landscape, a family somewhere. But then maybe it was never like that at all. Maybe it was he who was right. Her serenity was just a cynical acceptance of that condition of never finding home. Certainly not in nature. Certainly not in love, where all the time you're—well, what, exactly. Exposed in love; in its neglectful custody. On your way somewhere else, and always another.

HOW LONG HAVE I known exactly, she may find herself thinking.

Some weeks later: she is standing on the street, trying to smoke a cigarette, trying to become addicted to something. She coughs, her nose runs. She doesn't know if it's the cold or her having been left, her feeling more together by being totally left on her own. But everything is weeping, everything a collapse, a crashing down around her ears, a gash in her head, and she is as peeled; the sky descending around her, her skin. Utterly exposed in that way:

imperiled. Her head feels heavy, she bends backward and thinks: nothing lies heavy.

Nothing anyone can see.

She lies down on the flagstones, puts the cigarette down on the ground, from where it sends a thin coil of smoke into the air. She decides to lie there until the cigarette goes out. Or burns up. One of the two. And then she will let herself into her apartment again; and she lets herself in and finds warmth; she lets herself in, having managed to get to her feet, and then she lights her cigarette, and says: I've never smoked before, then speaks her name, and another man speaks his. Movements of that kind, taking place all the time, the kind of movements that can start going in reverse. Behind one's back. All of a sudden you're here again, or else you've never been here before. There you are; held upright by the suspicious cone of light from a lamppost.

THE WIND BLOWING in through the open windows smells like the sound of envelopes being opened with a knife. Seasons are nonexistent at the moment, in the days following the death of a friend. She gathers the shards, in her thoughts. The days cannot be told apart. Tomorrow already yesterday. She meets him for the first time. It is summer; I have finally come to say goodbye.

The keys of the apartment are as shiny as eyes too young for their face. I have lived inside you since I was eighteen.

Your face, when I am no longer there to see it.

I don't believe it.

A light, like darkness, all around you.

I let myself into the apartment. I lie down beside you on the bed. Or else I get into the bed between two sleeping figures. I push the other woman out. Sorry.

WE'RE JUST NOT happy, he told her. She went against him instinctively: yes, we are.

You're not listening to what I'm saying.

Yes, I am, I listen to everything you say. You're just not saying anything.

It was winter, he was lying with his back against the cold wall in her apartment. The apartment was on the third floor, on Løngangsstræde, backed up to the church, Vartov Kirke, sharing its spine. Sunday morning, and the room trembled, the clinking of the little candle holders and vases in the windowsill. The circular movement of the water in those vases, emanating outward from the stalks of the flowers; from the round eye of the vase, inward to the middle, a sky of new year—geometric patterns, tiny explosions without sound. The submarine rumble of the organ in the room. The hymn ran down the walls, Grundtvig's "Påskeblomst," the coldness contained in that. She thought of pushing him through the brick. He would plunge through the church like a beast. Or a bird with clipped wings. Landing heavily on ancient stone. Only the smell of vanilla and timber would discover his body.

Vast areas of loneliness, and of *alone here*. The edgeland, where the last houses in the village stand and rock their heads to the point of nausea, looking out upon the void, halted just in time—before the fields, plundered and plowed, made ready for, well, for what, exactly. Open land. A cry that may reach out across the landscape, and yet return to hit you full in the back. You will fall, perhaps, and then, perhaps, the houses will fall, too.

But they stand.

Trembling on the edgeland. Alone. A shift has taken place. They leave a party, and walk through the city. I'm cold, she says. The way he stops there, on the bridge. Takes her hands and pulls off her gloves, holds her hands up in front of his, in front of your, fleshy lips, fleshy and cracked, blowing warm breath against my fingers. Behind you, the tracks as they run beneath the bridge; your breath is moist and warm, and sheaths my white fingers like water.

We say nothing.

A car goes past. A train crosses beneath us, on the tracks under the bridge, it forms a crucifix, and we are in the middle. Your dreadful face is a caring face. What broke it.

When do you realize what these signs mean, a crucifix drawn beneath you. My eyes begin to water, it's the cold. You think I'm crying, and kiss me. There's a moment of togetherness there. We walk home, these two people walk home, a man and a woman, without speaking. Before they let themselves into the apartment, he holds her head in both his hands. She can hear herself breathing. The snow can do that: amplify sound. He leans in close, puts his face to hers, and places a kiss below her eye. The feeling of his lips as they touch, before he opens his mouth and licks the skin below her eye, licks the tears from her face, first one cheek, then the other; that kind of moment in time, the fact they exist. And that shift: toward something like words. We have emptied out, she thinks to herself. The noise of a bucket, jarring against the sides of an empty well. A horse, scraping the gravel, putting its muzzle to the ground and blowing, a cloud of dust, a hand feeling inside a dark box when someone has taken the last of the coins and there's nothing left for anyone. And one day it's like this: words in abundance, landscapes of them; a face dissolving into syllables: here underneath your nose is the apple tree from the garden at Agri, here is Svinkløv, here are the warm flagstones, everything drawn in outline, laid bare, the dots connected, the face a map: a picture book in which something is revealed, made visible. A person. But all the lines are stiff as wire; you move as if your clothes are still in the cupboard, in a pile: a slide, or a fall, perhaps, a body able—and then again: a body that doesn't even know what it wants, if it wants, anything other than to talk about—talk about what, exactly. Nothing. Most of what she tells him dissolves as it drifts from her body.

And then.

Where did you go.

She, who still sits on the floor under the sink, unlocks the door and lets him come in, and he falls around her like a loose dress whose shoulder straps someone sliced with a knife.

SHE REMEMBERS SHE was drinking that night. After she asked him to go. Are you sure you don't want me to stay. I'm sure, just go. She remembers knocking back one glass after another. As alone as could be, but nothing was the way one could imagine it to be: *right*. Nothing real. Or—too real by half. She wasn't quite grieving, but pretending. She was drinking, that's all. Because a person can do that. And because sorrow kept being postponed. By what. Canceled. By this feeling of nothing being real.

I'm not going to leave you, he'd said, more than once.

He was that ignorant, so it seems.

That young.

I'm just telling you like it is, that's all, he said, and then ran that eternal hand through his eternal hair. He kept revealing himself to be unhappy. Completely unsuited for life.

You leave people all the time.

You leave reality all the time.

She was angry, as if because of some unjust sentence, a match unfairly refereed, unfair weather and unfair fatigue.

The sun dangling from a thread.

Reality, riddled with sentences like:

I won't leave you.

It's not too late.

You never know what can happen. And yet we know all too well. We've known all along.

Can you remember when we met, he asked her later.

No, I can't. Can you.

Yes, he replied.

I don't think so. I think you can remember when we split up. It happened at the same time.

There is a sense of an approach in reverse. A body running backward. A mouth eating a piece of white bread into existence on an empty plate, drinking red wine until the glass is filled, raking chestnuts back across the floor, pearls, an inverse explosion; stripes on a candy stick appearing under the tongue. Collapsing, like a cake in the oven, one's thoughts, scaffolders falling like rain outside windows. That kind of disaster. That isn't insurmountable, as you always say. It all happened so quickly, we buried him. And the car, you should have seen the car afterward.

Unreal.

But it's not lack of reality that this is all about. It's just the world, when it gets *too* real. Like me, she thinks; maybe I was just too real for you.

You've been chewing your lip. Stop it.

Only he's the one who chewed his lip. That kind of mix-up.

It's spring already, summer already, autumn already, and winter has just begun. He has just begun; you have. She goes home and thinks about a child that never was. Herself, perhaps.

She is displaced in time, always.

HE SEES HER to the train and tells her about a film he saw. She thinks to herself his time will soon be short, she counts on the fingers of her hand, how many years, six years older than she, and for a moment she has no idea how old she is herself, but he is twenty-eight, that must be right. You think about children, you dream about children in the night and dream about them in the day. She knows he is thinking the plan is falling apart. And then he tells her about this Bergman film in which a young woman discovers that for a time in her childhood she hated her mother.

Autumn Sonata.

Only there was no place for that kind of emotion, he says. She looks at him, the lines around his eyes.

He throws up his hand. There just wasn't room, not at that time.

And later, he goes on with enthusiasm, the young woman kind of works it out. Realizes that the fear she feels all the time stems from this kind of—pent-up hatred.

She smiles. So now, she says, you think I should let myself hate my mother.

Yes.

She smiles. He smiles.

But that's not what I'm saying, he says. It's just something I've been thinking about.

I think it's the same for all of us. All Bergman's films are made for us all.

Maybe you're right, he says. Are you looking forward to going home to Mols.

She thinks for a moment. I'm looking forward to seeing if I *can*. If I can be there. I can't really be anywhere else.

I think it'll be a release for you, he says then. To get away from the city for a while. From that man of yours.

She nods. Perhaps. She kisses him suddenly on the mouth. Just so you won't forget me, she thinks. Hey, he says, and smiles. Hey, she says. I didn't mean it, she lies.

But then it was him kissing her, holding her tight. And then her turn to say hey, and he who lied himself to a kind of repentance.

Nothing is more or less real.

A particular kind of light she remembers from her childhood. A *realer* light, that makes everything look more real while it's there, and then afterward, when you think back: more *unreal*.

Are you coming with me, she asks him.

No, he says without hesitation.

Only she's the one saying no, and he asking if he can come with her. There's no answer.

No, is the question. No, are you coming with me. Are you coming with me, no.

She is a hunger artist, and only a single ticket sold. Her audience of one has fallen asleep. A balloon tethered to his wrist by a string, floating three meters in the air above. Inside a tent of busy stripes.

There is no solution to the riddle.

Look at me, he says, taking her hand. A month is nothing, you'll finally have peace to write. Or maybe he doesn't take her hand at all.

Peace and quiet.

Peace and quiet.

I THINK I am a person who sees everything that *almost* exists. It's a way of remaining unhappy, incapable in every respect. To see, not what *is*, but what *could be*. That which is coming, but which never comes, that chronic postponement, things imminent, likely soon, just around the corner, etc. Only sometimes it turns out that what lies ahead does not exist, there was nothing there, and I am someone else. *Almost* is the same as *not*, at worst *never*. Non-births, undesires, the impossibility of something like circumstances. *In any other circumstance*—it doesn't bear thinking about. I am a guest on her way home, reeling away from a party that never was. How come this intoxication, this hangover, these pangs of regret, when there wasn't even a party. Non-places. Whatever they are. It all starts and ends in an idea you eventually have to swallow. All your ideas and good intentions, that patience, that ability to convince the eye to see: invisible. And to be, fundamentally, seen—an invisible person in the world. To another, who cannot see you, cannot see me. Because he keeps disappearing anyway. Because he can't find the right distance: close. Because maybe he can't.

There are people who *cannot* love you. And it has nothing to do with wanting. It has nothing to do with desire. It becomes a matter of economics—negotiation. Columns, lists of one thing and another. A contract of service. Salary. Or no salary, voluntary work, driven by expectation and pictures of things to come. Like negatives, I see everything as though in negative, everything dark is light, and what's light vanishes into black. But you think you see a person. A resemblance. I see the outline.

But then it's not a person I see at all, not a person I expect. Who am I coming home to, who will be in my bed. A person in reverse, a person who *cannot*. Incapable. Incapable in love. And it has nothing to do with justice or ill will or the best of intentions. Love can be an economic specter, riding you through a series of images that never develop. Into anything. Other than images, an exquisite dream by which to sleep; from which to awaken bruised; what are you complaining about; you're almost there, at the finish line. And the excuses you're given along the way. Bait fed to you by corrupt animal keepers.

I forgive you everything; my body remembers it all. Going on is impossible; so, seemingly, is escape. It's already too late: when we met we died in each other's arms, in that very place; we died by that very look.

We drank each other like semi-poisonous drinks. Unthirsty. That is, I kept you until later. A later that never came; there was always something fatal about it. The truth is: perhaps there was something else too, though who can keep such things apart. That which is fatal, and, well, how to put it, love, perhaps. Serenity, perhaps, a home. It all short-circuits, thick belts crackling across the landscape: love, and something that can hardly be called love at all.

The fatality of *that*.

What you saw never being what you will ever see, those tiny disappointments, a thirst in need of a throat, following after us like a pack of stray dogs. And all the time the idea of what might have been: begging dogs, whenever you move to get up from a table, or leave through a garden gate, the past is waiting there. Undead, and not even past.

How naïve I've been, I think to myself. Or rather: how lonely. How *closely I scrutinized*, how clearly I saw it all in my mind—all that nearly was. The person who could love, almost; this almost-love, forever postponed, something else in its place. What, exactly. Reality. Whatever that is. Yours, I suppose.

THE
LANDSCAPE

WINTER. THE SNOW rumbling in still, without sound. Sometime after Christmas, I'm not sure.

The snow. That has laid itself upon it all, all that dares to remain exposed for more than a few seconds at a time, upon everything dead and everything living; the living and the dead; the violet stalks of the Brussels sprouts stand askew, keeping their balance in the broken rows of the vegetable garden, packed in by snow, as old wine bottles are encapsulated by melting, then stiffening candle wax, and the snow falls with the drowsy resolve of that image.

Obstinacy all around. We can't go anywhere. We are inside a house, and the house is a giant corpse. We lie here and wait, beneath the skin. Movements are agitated and take place indoors. Outside only when something compels one of us: to fetch wood for the fire, feed the birds, clear a path. Outside there is only snow and the flies. True, the fattest of the flies are survivors.

The roasting trays are by turn hot and cold. We girls stand and stare, crane our necks beneath the ceilings. Fledgling birds. Our mother, nearly burning the bread. It can still be done, in the old oven. Her lips tighten and she winces at the sizzle of wet cloth, the only thing she has time to put between her fingers and the hot tray. She burns herself, the skin blisters: the things I do for you, she says, a wry smile. The water runs from the tap, I am horrified. The two sisters each understand more or less than me, who understands exactly what is required to see the fatality of it, in that sentence. Blisters.

Nothing to be worried about, she says, comforting me, in that way. She means it, and yet her words are a weight to haul back into the boat, the clothes of the men are heavy with water, and we must sail on. Once more an about-turn; we always comforted each other *in reverse*; when I need comfort, when she does.

I think I looked utterly distraught.

The warm filling runs out of the sweet Shrovetide buns. The recipe book lies open on the table, *Karolines Køkken*. The filling of the buns, vanilla, and these rich yolks. I spell out the words on the title page, the Dairy Association's recipe series, the oddness of the subtitle, *Oh, Freedom*—someone must have been thinking of heaven, or something quite like it.

Sunday mornings at the Thorup Dairy. My eyes watering at the muslin cheesecloths, the dairymen slicing the blocks with wires. You can work in the dairy when you grow up, my father says to me. Perhaps that's where it comes from: the idea of your parents, for all that, not knowing you better. The disappointment of them not seeing the gravity of it. He hands me a slice of cheese, draped over his fingers, and I remember thinking of dog ears, the same feeling of body about it.

I hated the smell of sour milk, the swarming cheese. An army of holes. And I wanted to go in and yet not for anything in the world, to go in. The wind from the sea across the road sweeps across the parking spaces and me, a mad dog thrashing in its chains, I shake my hair and drag a comb of fingers across its ribs before clambering into the rear seat.

The bread has risen immensely, its back split open like a wound. The bread, the comb of its broken spine.

An old friend she has forgotten and suddenly recalls. My mother. She misses him, repeatedly. I'm not sure.

My lips are cracked. My thoughts.

My mother ties our hands behind our backs with her eyes, goes from the oven without closing it first; the oven issuing its heat into the kitchen. We try *not* to look each other in the eye. We glance about the room, our eyes are darts whizzing about the bread and the leaking filling of the Shrovetide buns as it sizzles on the tongue of metal.

The mother returns to her young in the kitchen again, interrupting them with her example: look, my wounded hands, she says. Holding them out in front of her. So that her offspring may inspect. The fledglings gather on the finger branches. They nod.

The tips of her fingers are swathed in band-aids. Ten little brown boxes on skin-covered bones. Their mother's hands, at least one joint in excess, as with each of her arms, each of her legs, shins, lower arms. And her bottom lip is twice as big, she has doubled in size.

Her hair is thick and glossy, wet slabs of molded blue clay. Her beaded bracelets rattle as her young once more look away. She is melancholy for three days, then busy for three, but her love is the same every day, quite insane and far more durable than anything ever before seen in this world. Her *remaining*. Something rare in that, that choice: remaining until—

Until what, exactly. Until the end. Until it no longer makes sense, until she is abandoned by us or by our father or by the feeling that in spite of everything there is meaning in the madness, the victims.

She puts bread and sweet buns in the freezer for the birthdays in spring. Her children were born in March, April, and May. If she's to be believed.

Sometimes I'm not sure, she can be so *absorbed*.

There is a fundamental lack of credibility about busy people, the way they insist on besieging dates and days and half-nights, annexing the world like that, colonially, with their own bodies. Come home for Christmas. Come home in good time.

Later, I'm like that myself, it's what all of us grow up to be, all three of us, in part, at least. At best there's something naïvely mendacious about that kind of vigor. At worst it's calculation, thinly veiled. So many important dates. So many children and even more mouths to feed and navels from which to pick the fluff. Giddyap, giddyap, all my horses!

Always this wish to be just as busy. As decent as our mother; we are watermarked. Maybe one day just like her, without these grubby, rural fingernails.

But our cuticles resist. My nails collect dirt. Earth is what they want.

I bring in some wood, a bustle of activity. A few seconds is all, and then a pillar of salt.

THE GOLD-THREADED bristles of a carcass poke up windswept, to be tumbled over the cloak of snow. So coarse, encapsulated each by frost, and the ice cap's desolate.

A slothful movement in the snow. Most things have given up and lie still. A slightness of motion every ten seconds. The world is giving a ball, and at each round an animal is selected, or a tree, or a person, who must leave the stage and retire to the wings with ears blushing. The ones who didn't move. Wrapped in hide of bison. The birds are in panic. No leaves remain to return the sound of their beating wings. No socks hung out to dry on the line, the metal hearts of the clothespins are glazed with pristine ice, frost blooms by turn on blue and red plastic. Posing arms of crystal. There is nothing like the echo of a world such as this.

I wake up with a snap abrupt as a wall, its beginnings a hesitation some hours after midnight. The wind switching to the east. The movement is an exact reflection of the slip of continental plates during an earthquake. Blankets of snow avalanching by turn. A shroud of matted marrow for the outer layer of the snow-cloak.

The sigh of the curly kale, its shelves of leafage.

Blankets that drop from plant cots.

An audible crashing-down. The smell of something giving way. Something else sinking slightly.

Crystal arms colluding with panes of glass, and something contracts and gathers in a droplet. A droplet plunges from the eaves to land upon the sunken head of a withered rose. The nod of the bush. My pillow has grown into my brain. She who is used to stained and lumpy pillows will fall asleep with her head in most any bony lap.

This infernal sound of droplets impacting and disintegrating. I wake up more fatigued than when I lay down to sleep.

ON THE LAST day of the year, my mother claps her hands in front of her chest, her eyes become tender mussels, orbs wedged tightly between lips of calcium. She enthuses—a rush of sibilants—about the grapes, Léon Millot, the ones she cuts in bunches from the vine in the greenhouse.

Being able to do such a thing. In December.

Winter all around. If this is not a miracle; if this is a miracle.

THAT WAS HOW I imagined it. That was what I wanted, to return here and to have a family of my own, in the village where we lived. The kind of face you see as you turn your head quickly inside an old house at evening, houses with such *sounds*.

There are images that will always occupy me. I have come to see them again, to be done with them again, or rather not, to not be done with them, ever. To continue being occupied. Continue *staying*, and yet leave.

YOU ARE PEELING an onion, you strike it hard against the chopping board and remove the outer layers with a large knife. Out in the yard they are slaughtering chickens. They ask me to fetch more boiling water in which to scald them, or polystyrene boxes to divide things up. A cow, half a cow. I vomit over the fence, into the pasture of sheep, my bile dangling like entrails in the windowed rectangles of wire, where it remains for some time before descending into the couch grass. Take her inside, someone says, and my mother smiles and comforts me. The onions, tenderizing in the pot. I find myself thinking you look like my father. You look like my father, I whisper. In the darkness you turn, sedated by fatigue.

What.

You look like my father, I say again.

They roll back to sleep. The kitchen sparkles, stars illuminate the bedroom. Can a room be dark and then so abruptly light without anyone having altered anything. The same stars in the sky, the same night.

You sigh; later, a whimper. To what kind of exile have you delivered me, your sleeping, sleeping body wonders, a wheezing enquiry.

What do you think. What do you want. But at the same time, I regret everything, approached by creeping nausea, the kind that reminds a person they knew all along and even savored the disaster's unfolding. I have a penchant for catastrophe. There is comfort in the sun always going down. The fact that in a way there is no hope, you know it is what will happen, and we can do nothing to prevent it. Death. I pick up a couple of blankets from the lawn, the dew has fallen, I tell myself, and again I am doing this too late (this is the kind of thing that makes me doubt I am no longer a child, and wonder if I will ever be anything else).

We drive through the plantation to Svinklovene. The roads are uneven concrete, massive slabs split like clay plowed up and frozen overnight, in the first frost. Lie down here. And the covering of morning: the world hushed, only the rhythmic snap of the flag-lines, pealing bells in the distance; and then we are at the harbor, some buckets put down in a basement somewhere, where washing machines idle—outside, everything is silent, like an odd shoe someone lost on the road.

Your body is accusatory, because I have taken you with me. That is your dream.

And yet you have no dream other than peace, so why blame me. Simple.

I SUPPOSE I had grown used to you, your being here; the sound of my own heart, the sound of a bush beating at the window all night, all day.

ONLY THEN IT wasn't you who had fallen asleep, and me lying sleepless; but the sound of me alone in a bed, and you turning in your sleep, beside a body that cannot find rest, a single movement that connects us all; me, waking as you turn, another woman getting up. It's not you, you will say; I just can't handle intimacy right now. I need—

Space, I say.

It's never one person leaving another; you leave each other, I think to myself. It takes place, a single movement; you have become one body, and this body falls apart. There is no blame to apportion, but accounts to be settled, and no one to send the bill to. All that I possess is yours. That kind of feeling.

The debts left by love. A single movement and you lose all, and must borrow everything. And thus it must all be carried about: everything that is yours, and all that you have lent out. A body like that.

SHE CAN'T REMEMBER beginning to love him, and she can't remember stopping. The feeling doesn't move like that, forward or backward. It exists, like a darkness that surrounds us, surrounding me. A desire for light, twenty-four hours a day.

Traversing the land to clamber up on Stabelhøj Hill.

The sky increasing in size, a sail unfolding above, the further one walks into the landscape. The cows are returning home, emerging from the pastures; it's that time of day, and their swaying udders are heavy and sore, pressed between their legs, weeping milk; the swarming flies that crawl upon the air, that find a settling place in the corner of an eye, a groin. The calves say nothing, they are knees that bend, and stiff hind legs, stilts brushing the tautness of the udder. Jets of milk spatter the earth upon every glance, liquid lingering a moment, pearls of purest white in the couch grass, then absorbed by the clay-like soil, beneath clovers of only three leaves. The veins of the mottled udders: blue. A woodland in which to become lost, a landscape that is not dark, not only. One could contend that all pathways are luminous. A lattice of trellis-work visible, holding a miscellany of wishes in place. You nudge me, to make me turn onto my side.

That's better, you say.

It's as if our bodies have melted together in that position, all other bodies to come are perfect casts of: this. Too much or too little body. I can't remember when we became more than two in this bed. But suddenly we were more, and I was someone else. Are you asleep, you ask.

IT'S RAINING, AS if there were a fire to put out, a steady downpour throughout the day, a recalcitrant blaze that will not succumb. When was rain ever a solution to anything.

THE FLIES ARE busy. They scurry across the walls of the kitchen, hasten across my sister's hand. She lets the hot water run in the sink, on the empty bottles with their stoppers.

Her hand, a surface of skin gripped by flies, is at rest on the counter.

Her other hand is reddened by hot steam. She holds them up to the light in front of her, the way you do with bottles of red wine, to see how much is left. She lets out a sigh, and stirs the pot on the cooker. The third sister has put her foot on the counter and is mending her laddered tights with garish nail varnish. From a tiny point of origin on the back of her footballer's calf, the ladder plunges toward the heel. Heavy drops of rain draw green streaks down the gray of the panes. The dripping from the tips of all the ferns after the rain. She closes her eyes and continues stirring briskly, so that her sister will not notice her and realize her disgust at the entire scene, the tableau of footballer's calf, nail varnish, kitchen.

Beneath her brittle ribs lies a conscience. On the cooker, she has shapely legs in one pot, elderflowers in the other. She always feels guilty about something.

DISTANCE HAS SHORTENED everywhere, no longer as far from one place to another since they cleared the trees. I go left, down through the wood that is no more. I think of you, decide to call you, but then to wait until later. That feeling I have: of always holding you off. I wonder whether the sentence can be inverted: if you have always held me off. And I—whether I took something in advance that ended up being canceled. I follow the stream, through the snow. I can't be on my own anymore, and I've only just started. It has nothing to do with strength, or lack of strength. It's about what makes sense. A friend writes me a letter, on this day of all days, he writes that you can't love a person who *cannot* love. I know he's thinking: because it ruins you. I'm not sure who I'm thinking about. Dead man. New man.

One kind of gravity colliding with another, that's what it is. Being home, and being nowhere at all. Being somewhere you know, without recognizing a thing. I walk the path into the woods. The hills are older, the woodland has advanced all the way up to the vertex; bald, sandy earth.

Does it mean anything, me walking here.

Maybe it means: you are walking here. No more than that. I want to call you, but I want never to call you again. The feeling that wells in me is of a celebration canceled. A number of people want to love me but are not allowed. A number of people cannot, or lack the courage. It doesn't matter. All there is here is this acute lack of home. The trees are bare, oak, I think. Yes, oak. A low carpet of self-seeded evergreen advancing to the trunks. They look frightened, as though, being caught red-handed on the point of some shameless deed, they lost their crowns in panic. You use me for thinking. I don't know what use I make of you, apart perhaps from survival. There is no one in the twilight here to notice that the trees and their crowns don't match. Evergreen and deciduous are different. And still I don't doubt that is what has happened: panic arisen among the trees, and sudden autumn. Leaf fall, a carpet of needles around the lower trunks, the feet of the oak.

BECAUSE LANGUAGE IS not innocent, but fire and weaponry. One wages war with words, risking all the time to fall into bed with the enemy. I'm not sure now, but that's what I thought when I got up and saw a boat come though the canal, towing the morning behind it on a rope. I'm not sure either if there is any pleasure in not being *compelled* to do something. And more generally: pleasure surely has little to do with such a thing as freedom.

SHE WAKES UP at his feet. Stares straight into them. She is lying on her side, and his feet are towers toppled in front of her collapsed eyes.

Her face is twisted askew and is made of dry clay.

Her face, fallen.

So big were his feet, then. So cold the room. He must have opened a window in the night. She remembers nothing of it. What she remembers is them not being able to reach, neither of them could reach. And then this: that he once lifted her up so that she might line the frames with shards of glass. To keep someone away, keep someone out.

The balloons are tired and shrunken after the party.

How distant it seems now: the celebration. And how unreal in this honest light.

He blocks out the sun with his foot. His feet have always been big, it strikes her now. Probably he is of another opinion. They see things differently, though mostly they are one body, one thought.

Look, she says.

He turns his heavy head toward her, a mechanical action, and she sees him against the light, a mane of hair edged by a nimbus.

His throat is a well, a rope hangs from the pulley, clutching a dismal zink bucket. Tomorrow once again, it will batter the lining of his infected gullet.

A wind howls in the well.

Her mouth fills with feet and jealousy.

If this is courage; this is courage.

She points, as well as she is able. Pokes a finger out in front of them. And it is as if he will not believe her; the little tug on her hand.

Come on, he says. Let's go home, let's go home where it's warm. The lake here will be dark soon. There are so many good reasons that only one needs mentioning. The dark, for instance. The others queue up in the mind, too many by far, like figures on the platform in Berlin, so many people soon to break up and be crammed into railway carriages. His woolly hat, always riding upward and back, and he, always pulling it down over his ears again unaware.

He puts his hands in the well to defrost.

Come on, he insists, and does not see the carp. They hang suspended in the frozen lake beneath them.

Carp-mouthed carp, the silver of scales.

She is more beautiful than me, she thinks, and collects her saliva, spits on the ice, and finally they go. The thought of it will not leave her, her spit descending through the ice like a drill, twisting its way ever down, a drinking straw of fish, a leggy man diving for pearls, to save up for the sake of some later amusement.

I GET OUT of bed and stand naked in the blue light. My feet seem unnaturally flat. It's like the original and the acquired have changed places. My heeled sandals missing, the soles of my feet are admitted to the floors.

THE APPLE TREE runs in through the window and along the hall. Its branches are trailing flames. The apples bruise against the walls.

The storm has woken me up.

The different sounds of the apples. The frozen red ones. Those succumbing, those rotten.

Branches swipe at furniture, stab at the pictures. The blue lithographs sway like street lamps, they buffet the wall, in the way of unknowing birds whose wings have been clipped. Helpless and inept.

If I can't identify the moments I live for, at least I can identify those I live in spite of.

Nature is disturbed by winter. I am, too.

MORNING HAS COME abruptly. Spring has arrived without them having noticed. Again, we are caught napping. She comes home and is quiet at the door as always. She knows to be silent. Her mouth is open, throat gaping, the air may come and go from her body as it pleases. Without sound. Her body is partition walling inside the apartment. She lifts and pulls the door toward her, turning the key gently, that certain way it must be opened so as not to creak. She is well inside the hall before she sees him. He is standing there, awake. Wanting to walk in the woods.

Good morning. Where does that smile come from. He walks beside her on the path, whose exultant green almost chokes on itself. They pass behind the amusement park, Tivoli Friheden, where everything as yet stands dripping the cold of night. Equal parts expectation and fatigue. And the leaves in the wind: a sound like gravel being raked.

He smiles, and she sees him against the light. He stands in the kitchen, an infant sun swelling behind him. Someone has moved the clouds. The traffic sounds different, the tire-noise belongs to brighter spring, brighter summer. In the summer you can hear the warm snap of asphalt.

She pulls off her running gear and showers. Reluctantly, she applies an extra layer of mascara. They walk in the woods, the anemones have pushed through the earth, are yet to unfold, though their buds are fat and glistening green. The light is unreal and renders everything: unreal. He talks, ignited with enthusiasm. His hands, his energy fill the entire clearing by the lake. She wonders if he even *sees* the woods. And if he does, whether they disappoint him, whether he will feel let down if he should look at them. An enthusiasm that renders everything unreal.

Someone told him about nature and now they are walking there.

The leaves have heard about the light, they unfold and present it to them. She waits for someone to extinguish him again. They will never be one with nature, but still they walk. It is as if the woods may be translated into portents and predictions.

Only they can't.

He is at least three different men, and she at least three different women.

YOU'RE SMILING, HE says, concerned. As though arriving home unexpectedly to find a table set for a candelit dinner.

Am I, she says.

She sits quietly, as if under a sky towering above fields at harvest, a cape of metallic blue to shroud the corn as it positions itself for the angry work of machinery.

AFTER EVERYTHING, HE visits.

It is afternoon, the weather is amazing. We ought to be out, she thinks. Nice chairs. Things you're familiar with. There are some clothes on her bed, some cupboards gaping, and all these books splayed apart. Look at this place, he says, and laughs. He says it's good to see she can allow herself to relax now. With things like that.

But it's my face you're talking about, she thinks.

It's her face he's talking about.

SHE IS STANDING in the kitchen, looking out onto the court-yard. Or else she is in her parents' kitchen, the budgerigars unsettled in their cage. The hedges are full of spring, the season resides now in the tiny feet and beaks of titmice and blackbirds. She descends into the cellar and retrieves the sun lounger. She finds blankets, and takes her duvet outside as well.

It's still too cold for anything, really. But still a person can lie down here, wrapped up in woollen blankets and duvets, in a spot of sunlight. There is sky, and there are windows cleaned, and nothing, but nothing in the way. The clouds travel across their backdrop of blue, and yet in an upward motion, ever more distant as one draws in the air. A shudder runs through your ribs, a feeling of demasking, a promise in all things—of clarity. No more talk. Everyone stops talking, work is done: sounds of a city at work. Posts hammered into the ground, duvets shaken in the air, the clatter of sundry objects dropped from balconies, the thunder of beaten rugs, a clicking of tongues, children reluctant to go back in and eat. And tomorrow the rain may come and draw its herringbone across the road in front of the house as drains gurgle. And he will perhaps be standing under the trees. As though waiting to be *consumed*. By nature. Because he is missing something and doesn't quite know what.

HE SAYS:

Sit down here a minute, meaning:

Summer is over, and the thought is unbearable. The apples, bright as eyes in the tree, little heads dangling from a belt. Summer, leaving without paying.

HER GAZE SWEEPS over the lawn. It picks something up. A little case of some sort. A bag of ripe redcurrants. The greenhouse perspires in a corner of the garden. The stalks of the tomato plants wilt after a long winter. You say there is nothing like tomatoes picked when red and ripe. The ones you buy in the supermarket are a different thing altogether. She borrows a car and drives out to the allotment gardens. No one has been there for ages. Perennials lie upon the ground. A single sunflower left standing, stalk broken under the weight of the head's heavy disc. Four wrinkled tomatoes hang bright as Japanese lanterns. Some things that need distributing between them. Everything that never turned out. Everything that never *happened*.

I DON'T THINK I want to move, she said. She remembers the way he lifted his head from his book and stared at the wall before turning round in the swivel chair and looking at her.

No, was all he said.

I'd have to sell the allotment.

He nodded, that was all.

She remembers thinking about a train, a train of non-sound, passing through a room like theirs, like light.

Then stay, he said. But I'm moving.

He barely packed a thing. She more, though not much. They leave each other without being able. A transition into something else. Doors unslammed. They have done this behind their own backs and realize only gradually that something impossible has taken place. The way it does, all the time.

SHE WAKES UP with the feeling of needing to go home. She tries to slither out from underneath, to rise from the bed without him noticing. She moves his left arm, which lies draped across her. Again, she has ended up here, a shifting tide backward in time. So they are trying again, once more there is hope of some kind. And yet it is a sorry hope, for each of them knows there will never be anything more than this. His arm: like opening the heavy wooden door of a stable in order to emerge into sunlight. He does not wake. It feels like he has borrowed his apartment from someone, there is something temporary about it.

And his face.

This is your face now. The way it changes all the time. I think I liked it better once. Always, liking better what once *was*. She puts on her clothes, open-mouthed, her body drawing in air without sound. She shuts the door behind her, knowing that she has no key. I will never be back, she thinks. She: the way she shakes her head when he holds up a spare set of keys in front of her one afternoon they meet at a café. Take these, he says. He, saying: take these, dangling them in front of her, the keys dancing like awkward adolescents held up by the scruff of the neck, legs like that. And her face, the feeling of not wanting them, of their belonging to someone else now. The feeling that everything has changed. And this pain of absence; how easy it is to miss someone, and how strongly. That desire to keep and conserve.

We can be friends.

But then maybe you can't stay friends without castrating each other. That's what she senses. He makes her incapable of loving others, and she does the same to him. She shakes her head.

Give them to someone else.

Has your new girlfriend got her own keys. She, asking him.

He shakes his head. He looks at the ground.

Give them to her. Then.

She gets up and leaves, walks out through the room; she thinks of her own apartment. The spare keys to her own place.

Where they are now. Berlin. In the pocket of her new man, who already has been buried, alive. In the arms of his own past, buried there in the woman he left in order to be with her.

She will ask him to return them. Perhaps they can be sent.

Only then she cannot bring herself to write to him. The fear of him actually sending them back. She goes down the stairs, her legs are pistons, she descends through the stairwell, taking all the air with her outside. She is assailed by the sun. She bends down and unlocks her bike. The particular chill of Frederiksberg in the mornings. She wheels the bike along Gammel Kongevej; changes her mind and walks back. She buys some bread at the bakery on the corner, where the light of the sun and the light of the city lakes collide like heavy girders, disrupting every face.

Again, she stands there outside his entrance. With bread inside a paper bag. The bag feels heavy, the bread rolls it contains feel like warm kidneys or hearts pumping. The body shares its rhythmic composure with everything that is dead. With bread. He looks glum as they sit there facing each other in the kitchen. Threadbare. She begins to regret coming back. Or coming back in order to leave in order to come back. She doesn't really know *what* she regrets. She doesn't really know what has worn her down. She has all sorts of thoughts about it, only they go off in different directions, first this way, then the other. She doesn't trust her own emotions. They come to her and leave her again in all their dictatorial arbitrariness. A person can tire of never understanding *how* things happen. Or you can become fatigued from knowing all too well what it takes. Knowing, and yet at the same time knowing it will not happen. That the option isn't *available*. His mind is a conglomerate of basements, she sees that now. Literally. Inside are corridors, rumbling echoes as the watchmen run through them at night, high on morphine. Maybe he doesn't know, but he hopes I will come back. This is what she thinks. A victory march.

So she thinks.

That he misses her. He gets up and goes over to the fridge, fetches something, or nothing at all, then sits down opposite her again. He places his hand on top of hers on the table and they look into each other's eyes. Or else they look down at the table.

IT'S STRANGE, HE lies, I never miss you when you're not here. I get so scared I might forget you, he tells her. He has talked her into meeting. I'm beginning to forget you, he says. That's the way it's supposed to be, malicious voices tell her, only these are her own thoughts, they carry her signature. And presumably it is what he wants, or what a person dreams about at night; dreams about during the day, not wishing it upon one's worst enemy. They walk there together, in the park by the National Gallery. It is summer and they are constantly on the run from someone. Both of them seeing someone else now, and one of them always wanting to try again. But only one.

He tries to explain to her that they are standing at a crossroads. He extends his fingers and turns his hands into stiff tools, crosses them on top of each other. An intersection, he says. They both look at his hands, and he lowers them again. They walk around the city for hours, drifting like a plow through endless fields of America, following the highway or cutting cross-country. Drawing a trail of moist soil behind them like snails, through shaded gardens, cultivated landscapes gouged open to the flesh.

I don't believe in you, she says.

He looks at her and asks what she means. And then they are silent for a long time, walking through the landscape that Copenhagen sometimes can be.

It's a very beautiful day, she thinks.

Sometimes it can be that simple.

THE MORNING COMES from below. It is summer, and the
air is static, embracing everything, warmth and light. She recalls a
morning at Agri when she awoke refreshed from sleep, the feeling
of having slept *sufficiently*. Immediately, she knows they have gone
off without her, that she is there alone. The sounds of the house are
undisturbed. No one to encounter, no sisters to disturb the life of
things, a life that hums and emits noise in its own quiet way, a bit
like words whispered under a door, through a keyhole: please open
up and come out, so we can talk about it all. She gets up and her
blue nightdress falls into place around her body. She pads on heavy
feet along the corridor, the doors of the other rooms wide open
like graves plundered by robbers; the beds, these empty boxes, the
stairs. In the kitchen, a shaft of light picks out half a cucumber left
on the table, crystals of ice encircling the seeds. Or perhaps they are
crystals of sugar, a staring eye, dissected blandness of water, a shim-
mer. A tea bag, trapped by the lid of the pot, the table stained by
its dripping. She picks up the cloth that is already there, still damp,
and wipes the table, wipes away the stain. She goes over to the
French doors, the sun strikes her face. At this early hour, the hill
delivers its measure of shade to the house. The door is not locked,
but the handle is turned upward as if it were. A barrage of sound,
she opens the back door, a barrage as she opens the door, like a rush
of water, finding its way and consuming a home; the grass is cold as
a church, and wet, crying out that it is summer, as though it were a
seldom occurrence, as she walks over the lawn in her bare feet. The
garden: a detonation of green, white, yellow.

The lilac bushes are in bloom, at their peak.

She wonders where they have gone. They have left her behind
in a world of her own. A feeling of missing out on something, and
at the same time a sense of having won a prize.

The past does not come creeping in the form of images, it's there all the time, tugging at your sleeve, trailing along behind you, occasionally wanting to be lifted up and *carried*.

A chinking of bottles from carrier bags suspended from handlebars. The street lamps are cupped hands. Ready to be filled with rain again. She lives in Copenhagen now, and is on her way home. A celebration folded up and put away in her mind. She could sleep all through next morning. All she needs is to drape a sheet in the window. Strange nocturnal voices sprout at every corner, their pale, near-transparent roots encroach, offshoots striving upward like hair made electric. A drunken babble on high, bodies plummeting, no time to reach out and break one's fall, faces hurtling toward the ground, buffeted by doors and windows that open and shut. This entire hall of mirrors, with its outside and in, its being in transit, and *where have you all gone*. The summer's parties and homelessness, the *coming from below* of this morning. Distant days repeat through the cracks. And again this light, this light, again.

BENEATH MOSS THEY find the False Chanterelle. Here, he says with pride. Yes, she says. They leave fairy rings, their tramping about. Apples fall. And leaves. They still go home together, intentions seemingly still the same. The warmth that consumes you, rising up inside you, when you're standing in the kitchen and have been outdoors the whole day. The feeling of hunger, absorbed in the steam of mushrooms, butter and cream, a nausea and satiety of a kind that has nothing to do with either food or no food, but with expectation and having walked through woodland, that peculiar kind of concentration so reminiscent of reading: attentiveness, and its exact opposite. To command large areas of forest floor, survey the ground as though it were soup to be skimmed of impurities; to find the mushrooms that are there. Searching for something in particular without knowing exactly what. Proceeding toward a place that exists only as movement and direction.

IN A CORNER of her garden, the greenhouse, like a dead man, the warmth of life yet to leave the body. She hears him, weeding the path with the hoe. Now and then he pauses, perhaps to remove some more stubborn plant, to pull up the root. Getting rid of. Or else to wipe his brow with his T-shirt. He leans the hoe against his chest, gripping the hem of the garment with both hands, lifting it to his brow, wiping so that the sweat will not run into his eyes. Or else he rummages in the shed, to mend the roof where it leaks. He tidies the raised beds. Or else she is alone and it is later, and the sounds he made hang like voices out of windows. Long after he is gone. Always, this feeling of long after.

HE WALKS AS if his every step is an item he finds on the ground and decides to pick up. Some movements in the ranks, some of us switch spots and will be next. Washing hangs from the line between the trees at the far end of the garden. It is the first time this year they have been able to dry their clothes outside. She walks with her mother through the garden, up the slope. The light is warm now. She closes her eyes and turns her head, the sun falls upon her face.

She stands a moment.

Her woolen sweater prickles at her throat.

But her face.

That's right, she says. Summer has yet to come. That sense of new beginning. You know it won't last, in fact it is gone the very instant you sense it to be there. Always something catching up with you—always something that is already too late.

We are taken unaware by the blossom of white, the yellow of the broom, and then the pink, and before we know it we are bathing in the lake, piling into cars with towels wrapped around us, already on our way home from the year's last swim, the lake freezing over, frozen over, the summer sealed inside, letters sealed with red, and it is Christmas and well into the new year before you even realize Christmas is gone, summer is gone, what happened, and where are we now.

NOTHING DRIPS. RHYTHM of that sort does not exist. Not below freezing. The sound of frost is the same as the sound of polished boots standing lustrous on an unread newspaper in an empty, white room. Unused shoes without laces. They have agreed to meet on her birthday. Nevertheless. The way they always do. Besides, there are some matters he wants to discuss with her, he says on the phone. She has a strong feeling it would be best not to see him at all. She knocks over a vase of sprigs and lilac. The smell of stagnant pond. The water runs across the shelf and drips onto her books. One of those accidents that make her give in and go along with him, in spite of what she feels. It's my birthday, after all. She pulls the damp towel from her body and places it on the shelf. She shakes the books one by one, wiping the covers dry with a corner of the towel; flicks the pages and leaves them to dry on the windowsill, opened out like fans. They look like stuffed birds with outstretched wings, about to—well, what, exactly.

SHE HELPS HIM into the shower. He is feeble and slack, and though her sleeves are meticulously rolled up she is quickly soaked. She talks to him. About the soap, about whether he is able to stand on his own while she washes his hair; she tells him to be careful and not to fall; she says the lather is rinsed away now, and asks if he can dry himself or wants her to help. His eyes flicker, he is angry, but too tired to do anything about it. Sick, and incapacitated by alcohol. She rubs his hair with the towel.

He gets up, it is well into the afternoon and she isn't there.

The apartment is empty.

He stands in the last rays of sun as they slant weak warmth down between the roofs of the buildings opposite. He imagines Arizona, fields of maize, grasshoppers consuming unscrupulously. She has a feeling inside her, as though she were separating an egg, passing the yolk from hand to hand, the fragile yolk that might break at any moment. She remembers all the objects she has broken. A small vase. A cup he gave her once. A glass that stood out only on account of being green in a particularly detached and dusty kind of way. Stand still, he says. She gathers the shards in her hand. Stand still, he says again, this time with annoyance. You'll cut yourself. I won't cut myself. That evening he tells her he thinks her parents scolded her unduly as a child. For breaking things. That had to be why, the reason she gets so upset. But it wasn't like that at all, quite the opposite, she thinks to herself. She finds it unreasonable not being allowed to be saddened by time passing. By doing things that cannot be undone, by suddenly dying. That is what a person cries over when they break a glass—no more than that, spilled milk, borrowed time.

He wakes up alone in the apartment, most of the day gone. She is out buying groceries. But how is he to know. He thinks she is angry, but she cannot be angry at all. Disappointment is a greater, more satisfying revenge, one may think, and perhaps it might be true.

JUST THE FACT of getting away from the city. They stay in a summer house. She reads Tove Ditlevsen and thinks of all the similarities. How alike people can be, across all boundaries. He sits uneasily in the shade of the parasol. The fabric lends his face an oddly blue tinge. A newspaper has blown from the table, some hours ago now, and has disintegrated, its pages draping the shrubs, covering up the dry straw. What remains lurches through the garden, like an army in dissolution, soldiers searching for survivors. Are you thinking about your mother, he asks her. They look at each other. She gives a shrug: not really. She'll be all right, he says, and looks down at his book again, only then to go on, how remarkable she is. You mustn't think it's you, you mustn't think that at all. But I haven't done anything wrong, she tells herself; you haven't done anything wrong, he tells her. She nods.

There's no one here, she whispers. They have come through the back garden, through the gap in the hazelnut, behind the house and the woodshed. Everything has been left so *neatly*, the dishwasher emptied, the table wiped. They have walked all the way from the summer house to Agri. But no one is here. They find some fizzy drinks in the fridge and sit out on the patio. Only that doesn't feel right either. They feel like burglars. She hangs the key back where it belongs, on the nail under the eves. He sends messages to Copenhagen, a couple each day. She doesn't care. It may be a bad sign, and she thinks about that. We'll give it one last chance, she hears him say, mostly for his own benefit; it's like he can't be talked into anything, the sheer impossibility of him. And then coffee, drowsiness, exhaustion, perhaps the heat. They chink glasses in a toast. They drink, and make love, and live their separate lives, together again in the midst of the summer, in this recollected landscape, this recollected summer house. Do you remember this, remember that, the time I nearly broke that window helping your parents pull down the old cladding. Always the disputes of chronology, for which reason it's easiest to leave it out when reminiscing, together. Where does that thought come from: that they are only together because they can't stand the thought of having forgotten something. An odd mistrust of memory, an odd displeasure at its existence.

HER MOTHER SQUEEZES her hand. Sometimes it's hard to understand, she says. She thinks she does, and yet tries to see the incomprehensibility of it. She stays with her parents for a few days, it is the winter holiday, they were supposed to have been together, she and the new man, the dead man's successor, the nocturnal worker, while everyone else sleeps, a moonlight contract, the body refusing to give up anything at all. But only she is here. She keeps waiting to be, what—unhappy.

However it may look, that kind of *sorrow*.

The sofa is so deep you either have to sit on the edge and not lean back or else succumb with legs outstretched. She feels the springs through the fabric of the upholstery, hears their metallic complaint as she settles into place.

Her father comes home and nothing about him seems changed. He is the same person, though there is no guessing who. His moods are arbitrary, as if they depend only on themselves, regardless of circumstances. The time his father died, her mother gathered her daughters on the old red sofa, their legs dangling above the floor, it is as if all the furniture has grown smaller since then, the gardens shrunken, unlike nature, oddly enough, whose proportions are unaltered; wild. She told them Daddy very likely feels sad, that's the way she put it. That they were to show consideration and be nice to him. And yet he came home and there was nothing to be detected, he was no more broken, no more repaired than usual, one minute at ease, the next quivering with tension. That constant unpredictability. I come home, abandoned by a man who passed through my hands and died; I come home, abandoned by the new man, and on neither occasion is he moved by it. In the midst of my doubting I will ever be alive again, or even want to be; I think to myself that in a way it ties us together. Both of us unpredictable. A rhythm that remains the same, regardless. A threat. They have already parted, or else they will never part. Nothing new under the sun.

SHE PRACTICALLY STOPS eating. Hardly anyone is concerned about the fact, and then suddenly they are worried sick. They travel to Italy, she and a girlfriend, and she perspires until thin, up and down the hills of Cinque Terra, in the streets of Levanto, where spring is coy and reluctant. It is the coldest spring in forty years, at least, says the eldest brother in the family-run hotel on the coast of Amalfi. They are the only guests, *their* guests. They sit in the café on the edge of the cliff, the sea its tall baseboard of blue. He tells her, as best he can in his own peculiar variety of English, that his parents are dead, that now only the three brothers remain. They don't think they can afford a room, and are allowed to put up their tent on the patio in front of the house. He unlocks the door of an annex, leaving it open so they may creep in to sleep at night. The extravagance of the blue sea, Italian espresso maker in chrome and shining red, men in attendance. The Italian wants her to guess how old he is, but she doesn't want to, she knows he is over fifty. He pulls a chair out at her table and sits down. She has no newspaper from which to glance up, nothing to put aside, and instead must rearrange her napkin. His lips begin to speak before he utters a sound, he wants to take her sailing with him, he says. Tonight. Fishing, he corrects himself. She dares not, declines, and feels she has never regretted anything as much ever before; the night that could have been.

A SINGLE ROOM. A bed beneath a window, a desk, their suit-cases gaping. Her dress on the chair; and he on the bed, in the shade. The doorway teetering, a slab of hot light. A little window facing the sea. The Amalfi Coast. The sun is high, the rented room dark and cool. From outside they look like lovers.

She goes out onto the terrace and leans over the railing, is gid-died by heat and altitude, the sea crashing against the rocks below, atomizing into spray, vomiting its white insides. He comes out and stands beside her, a bottle of wine in his hand. He drinks from it without any semblance of elegance, the slosh of its contents as he tips back his head to swallow. He goes back in and lies down again; he is tired, but cannot sleep. How can anyone sleep in this heat, he asks.

How can anyone do otherwise.

The roads here are gouged from the cliffs, half the time they lead through tunnels in the rock. The sudden astonishment of a view, a division of travel into dark and light, twisting the twine of day into rope of two continually interchanging complexions. He couldn't be bothered to leave, and she wants to stay here forever. But the next day they pack their suitcases and head on as planned. There are no birds here, he says. Yes, there are, she says. They are sitting in a bus on the way to the train station. No one knows how long they must wait there.

IN NABOKOV'S *LOLITA* there's a scene toward the end where the brutality of desire is revealed in a glimpse. It's when the reader and the main character see Lolita, there in the bathroom, her dis-tress. At once, a darkness is cast upon all that came before. You realize you've been seduced. You see yourself in that mirror, humbled, because you couldn't see any better. Again, you have involved yourself in something you didn't believe existed.

THEY MEET IN the sun one morning. He has just opened up the second-hand bookstore he's taking care of for a while. She gets off her bicycle and wheels it along to the little café table and the chairs they've put out front. You can get coffee there, and sit outside.

This is nice, she says, and gives him a measured hug, as though she were afraid he might fall inside her if she held him too tightly for too long. Their bodies: open wounds that may join up and heal as one if they're not careful. A merging of tissue, like plants climbing a trellis to arch across a garden path, across disorder.

Congratulations on your . . . success, he says.

She bows her head, gaze fixing the ground to make her seem shy; then slowly she unfurls and looks him in the eye. She doesn't know what success he's talking about, but she knows he means the book. As if that meant anything. It means nothing to her, not now. Thanks, she says, emptily. It's not like I got the Nobel Prize or anything, she says.

He shrugs and says congratulations anyway. Just getting published is reason enough.

She shrugs. Thinks: what kind of sadness is this. All the leaves of the linden trees are pale, the sun is drawing the color out of everything. They don't speak.

Do you want to see my window, he asks her, sweeping out his hand. She leans the bike against the wall. Duras, Jelinek, J. P.

Jacobsen. Some nice publications that look like exercise books. A tattered Taschen, Picasso. He has angled them carefully, wanting it to look accidental and yet alluring. Two books, one at each side of the picture, have been leaned against supports. She smiles and nods; nice choices, she says. He is so enthusiastic about the display, she sees, and hopes not a book will be sold from out of his window today. That it all may stay the way it is and be resplendent.

HE IS STRETCHED out on the sofa with one leg draped over the backrest. It is morning. Drowsy from sleep: when did you get home. His bare foot dangles like a wilted child in the sun. It is summer, seven o' clock. His face is covered by a blanket; she lifts it gently, startling them both; I thought you were asleep, she says in a voice that is quite emptied of voice. Breathless. Seamlessly, she lets go of the blanket and puts her hand to her mouth. What happened, she whispers, alternately pointing and putting her hand back to her mouth; his face is streaked with dried blood, in places near-blackened, in the creases around his eyes. Violet. And his face then moves, first the eyes, tentative and with scepticism, as if the muscles themselves do not believe movement to be possible. He groans, and furrows his brow as if to rouse his face. He shifts his weight awkwardly, like a piece of heavy furniture, and she recalls the time in Berlin when he wanted to get in the bath tub with her, drunk; the way he looked like furniture then as well.

Alcohol makes people into furniture.

Dependent on others to move them about.

What happened, she asks again. I walked into a cupboard, he

sighs. She can't help but laugh, only then to fall silent as a fire quickly smothered. She nods and leaves him on his own. She runs her usual route beside the sea, passing the Varna Palæet, following the path around the point, down the steps to the bathing jetty and the changing rooms. She writes her name in the book and finds her towel, pads serenely to the end of the jetty, the morning is quiet here. She immerses herself in the sea, and afterward she sits down on the edge of the wooden structure and dangles her legs. The planks make a bench; it's March and they're already lined by bodies, pale and doughy, slowly reclaiming life, bodies walking down the jetty and back again. A switch occurs in her mind, and she imagines nocturnal corpses, drifting in the swell, gently buffeting each other at the first sand bar, in the gloom beneath the jetty, wherever the current will take them. The woman next to her has only one breast. She imagines the missing breast floating amid the night-heavy corpses. She tells the woman about her morning. Perhaps to correct the imbalance of her mentally having encroached upon this unfamiliar body's domain without having first been invited in. If such accounting is possible.

So you fill in the ledger, and then burn it. Didn't he need stitches, the woman asks without drama. She shrugs, spilling coffee on her thigh. I suppose he did. She gets up and goes into the changing room, calls home. He doesn't answer, of course he doesn't. She runs through the woods and gets him into a taxi to the ER.

SHE TAKES OFF her shoes and puts her feet up on the dashboard; they are driving too fast through the Swedish forests, Småland, on their way to the eastern skerries, the Sankt Anna Skärgård, fleeing from the mosquitoes further inland, the melancholy of that remote former smallholding lay like a dropped undergarment around one's feet, thick ribbons of mosquitoes blowing in from the lake. It is summer, we can sleep in the car or under the trees, stricken with the fever of the season, a sense of this never coming back, and at the same time the comfort of that, the fact of everything soon reaching an end, on account of it not being *real*.

If anything ever is.

Without you I wouldn't have survived a day here, she thinks, I would have died of homesickness. The AC blasts its air, her skirt billowed about her midriff as she tries to find a radio station, as she tries to love him for some other reason than necessity.

WINDOWS THROWN OPEN, something else to come, and the thought, in the mornings especially, of everything now in flux, the sky above us is different, and the light, a totally different light, settled on all things that surround us. Our legs, in that light, as if finding sheen, the glow of shoes on newspapers outside front doors, scuffed boots polished by sun, laundry basket gilded on the tiles of the laundry room. Health. The fact of you lifting your legs a little higher when you walk, the fact of you wanting to come, of saying yes, that would be nice; and the fact of her once again dropping something that smashes into pieces and cannot ever be repaired, and there being no point crying about it. He has this idea, and asks her to help him move the sofa over there, just to see what it looks like, to see what it does to the room. All of a sudden she feels so tired, she thinks to herself, and lifts the sofa with him, carries it across to the other side of the room. It looks like it's trying to escape.

That's it, he says, and takes up various positions, viewing the arrangement from all angles. It makes her think of cattle auctions, or just the horse trader from Femmøller, this act of appraisal, though without their sceptical point of departure, with an enthusiasm instead that seems to her like a tribute to everything there is, but which perhaps in actual fact—this is the feeling she has—is the exact opposite. A way of *not* seeing what is. He claps his hands together, a crack of sound. So what do you think, he says, already on his way to the kitchen to make coffee; and everything is already the same.

THERE ARE TWO tight bundles of images and recollections; have I told you this before, he asks. Yes, you have. He slows down, holding up the traffic, leans over and points: that's where I used to live. And that's where I worked once. The warehouse, how hard was that, a warehouseman, and he tells her once again about their fingers in winter, having to wear those gloves with the fingertips cut off, never exactly knowing if it was so they could work the machines more safely or because the gloves would wear out at the fingers anyway. She stares stiffly through the windshield. She wishes they could drive quickly through a landscape that is unfamiliar to her. A fleeting face without history. This disinclination toward him, that in actual fact is an allegiance to the love she still awaits.

SOMETHING ABOUT HIS face. It snowed again today. The sun never arrived in the sky, it was as if something were holding it down at the other end. All of a sudden she thought he looked like the few other men she had been with. She felt like there were too many of them in the apartment. And the feeling of she herself being someone else, that she likewise was a number of other women. He sits slouched over his books; she kneels beside him and grips his thigh; he swivels the chair, and she crawls between his legs. Puts her arms around him and buries her face in his crotch. He strokes her hair. The winter wouldn't leave: every time you thought spring had come, snow came instead. No cars on the roads. Jobs made to wait. The ground is frozen: you can't plant the bulbs, or bury a friend, all you can do is stand around and wait, for all your good intentions of getting things done, and a new face every day, no matter what.

THEY WHEEL THEIR bikes along the canal. They talk about going swimming, but know it won't be today. It's late afternoon, she senses an imbalance in the picture, she gets up so late, and it's as if she's going forward in the wrong lane. Everyone is going *home* from something. Her younger sister is exhausted by work; says there's no time to be unhappy. She nods. I can see that, she says. It might be easiest that way.

Her sister is offended and hides it badly. She herself doesn't know how it feels to be angry in that way, it's like there's always been this great pool of emotions and characteristics to be shared out between the two sisters, and no one has ever bothered to divide up the individual emotions, split the pile fairly into two equal portions. She says she's convinced it's because of her book, those scenes from *home*. That whole *project* of yours. What is, she asks. Mum having cancer, he sister replies.

That's the sort of thing people with cancer say, she says.

The two sisters sit down on a step to drink sodas. She says nothing, puts the bottle to her lips, tilts her head, puts the bottle down on the woodwork.

Is that what you think, she says—I say—eventually. Is that what you think.

It's what they say, says my sister. That it's usually psychological, triggered by a depression, or some enormous grief.

I nod without knowing one way or another, rocking my head like a weaving horse.

There's a crane on the other side of the canal, lifting rust-red plates of metal from the cobblestones onto the bed of a truck. Dangling sheets of iron, delivered like well-aimed slaps to the face. The blue sea, a blue belt dissecting the picture. The crane is a strong arm slashing the sky. And then the feeling of discarding masks, of coming home. I'd like that.

I HAVE NEVER before wanted anything, she understands that now. It's not a competition, you say, meaning: I can't stand to lose anything more.

THE
NEW
MAN

WE MEET BRIEFLY, he's with his girlfriend and son. Copenhagen's Nørrebro district late morning, it must have been autumn, though still with summer's remains, making everything a matter of postponement. How long like this. Borrowed time. I'm wearing a red dress, black wellingtons. He doesn't need to see any more than that, even in that instant he has already seen too much. His gaze, indiscriminate: seeing what soon will be possessed, and all that must thereby be renounced; images assail him like a blazing pack of hounds dropped from a loft aflame, and we are drenched, saturated by fire and body. Something on the verge of happening, something already happened, something painfully absent. He greets the musicians, leans a guitar and a saxophone case against the wall. All the time, his eyes are on me. And his girlfriend sees it all, though in reverse, a mirror image reflected in all surfaces: a gleaming eye, a polished boot; and in that way it is enfolded, in the look in his eyes, and we tear off each other's clothing, the three of us there, inside the storm, a morning dawned upon an island from which we must depart on different ferries; no time to say goodbye, an uncertainty as to where we stand, now, and to what it means; a disenchantment,

a sudden degeneration of substance, a feeling of having staked everything on a horse, only for it then to abandon the race, a sense of
the entire world being a trick, everything *fixed in advance.* And in
that same gaze I put a phone back into my pocket in the parking
area outside the former slaughterhouses of Vesterbro, telling myself
out loud that it's best that way, to give him time, knowing full well
that there is no time, that time is past; the beginning and ending of
everything in one insane displacement, a cloudburst, the rip of an
awning, its sudden deluge. This is how it is again, this is how it is
that morning in the rehearsal space: some flowers whose stems you
cut and place in water; the same stems are dry and withered as you
break them in the middle, stuff them into an empty milk carton
you then drop into the bin under the sink; something you hope for,
and something you regret, a single displacement, a continuing drift
toward the center. A core, that nevertheless can never be found; a
reverse explosion of life, a reverse explosion of death.

He puts out his hand and introduces himself by name. I do likewise, only to realize that instead of telling him my own name I
have repeated his.

His girlfriend walks up the stairs to the stage, where I am placed
on a tall stool in front of a microphone. There is something wrong
with the sound, a squeal of feedback as she steps up. She hesitates,
tiptoes almost, ducks her head slightly between her shoulders, an
apology. She comes toward me and I point the microphone away.
Hi, she says, extending her hand and introducing herself. Her hand
is cold, but mine is colder. Are you a singer, she asks. I shake my
head. No, I say.

I smile. She smiles back. She is so warm and friendly, she takes
my hand and clasps it tight. As if we're going to have a life together.
Only we're not, I think to myself; perhaps we're going to share

one. Half for you and half for me; not a whole life for either of us, not a whole man.

When they leave, he carefully closes the door behind them. I can't help but smile, for there's something involuntarily symbolic about the world at that moment: him closing the door so carefully—as if you can close a door.

The body remembers.

A dead man, who will never again be alive for you, but who will continue to breathe his breath into your face without end. And all your kisses will taste of something that *was*.

He walks at your side, the dead one, sheet-white skin, sheet-white eyes, sheet-white orbs, apples, dangling like droplets. And snow. It is the mind that forgives; the body does not. The body bears its grudges, a maudlin procession of things past, a mourning in the streets. Marrow and bone.

YOU'RE SO YOUNG. Is what she sees the new man thinking. About her, her being so young. Later, he tells her this, though by then it is a repeat, for she has already heard him think the words. They are in her apartment: you're so young.

She studies him. Sighs and then tells him what she feels to be the truth: that she doesn't think it's important. That she has tried to think it is, but simply can't.

He nods, the same serious expression as hers, accepting the gesture of her nod, as if it were a plate being passed around for the second time, an unconscious plate.

She realizes she is smiling.

She cannot stop herself from smiling, because the thought is beautiful and so heartrendingly naive. It is like placing a sheet over a naked body, allowing friends to search the room, and then to stand there in the doorway afterward, guilt-free. Cleared by a lie: if only we are quiet, offer up our empty hands; and then to encounter this peculiar form of discretion. A will to see the island of bones on the bed through fanned-out fingers that desire not to expose, eyes that will not *see*, for seeing is an obligation, whose nature remains unclear. And who knows if there is time, perhaps they will prefer to leave in the interim, never to witness the grand finale, the conjuring forth of corpses.

I WAS YOUNG when I fell off a horse and damaged some cartilage. I understood something about the body then, realizing the way the thighbone ends at the knee. Your crumpled cotton shirt shares its colors with the pigeons and the bellies of the sky, the sky as it hangs upon the hills again today—these saturated curtains, and unsettled fogs, bluish breasts, falling as rain.

I wonder again if all your reservations about me are in actual fact the closest you can get to telling me you never wanted this. I never asked for any of it, you whimper in sleep.

The work your body does each day is touching.

You are the most touching thing I know, your lack of *serenity* moves me. Your looking for ways to push me away from you is touching in a way that has nothing to do with morals or not, nor with responsibility, nor even love, I suppose. Your guilty conscience squirms inside you. I don't know if you're telling me the whole truth. But then maybe that's just how it is, all the time. The truth constantly in flux, and whatever you tell me is true, and everything squirming inside you is, too.

Have you told her, I ask.

You nod, only then to shake your head. I don't know what to say to her.

I try to convince you you don't need an excuse not to love someone anymore, that you don't always have that kind of explanation to provide.

We walk through the city and find the only restaurant open so late. For a moment, you actually look happy.

Thanks, you say, and squeeze my hand under the table.

For what.

You're right, I don't need an explanation, I can tell her it's not her fault, it's just me. Or you.

I smile at him, and my face; it must have looked dreadful.

You're beautiful, you say, a whisper almost. Do you know that.

I shake my head, my dreadful face, one of those autumn leaves, where you pull the tissue from the veins, and the ominous skeleton that's left.

Who am I then, am I someone else now. There is a repetition in the world, and it rides around on the most disquieting steeds; ominous as hell itself. The slightest movements are reflections of the very largest; desolation exists, the betrayer, too, the deception.

I'm unsure if we can ever speak again.

I LAY WITH my head on my new man's chest. It rose and fell, as unsettled in sleep as from the moment of awakening. I thought about the deckchairs outside. I remember this: waking up a few minutes before him, and the weight of the arm that lay on top of me. A collapsed ceiling. Buried alive, the serenity that must be a part of that, regardless of all else. Having only so much oxygen, a few helpless gasps and one final breath.

When morning came we walked along the shore, crossing some black stones embedded in the green moss; it was as if nature had cultivated itself, and yet one couldn't help thinking it was so exquisite, the green and the black, that it couldn't have been cultivated at all, for cultivation presupposes thought, and the uncontrived beauty of this was so *convincing.*

What is it with you and Berlin, I asked him.

He looked down so as not to stumble, or else he looked down so as to avoid looking at me; I live there, he said after a moment. My son's mother lives there; my son lives there.

And then I was the one looking down.

He *lived* in Berlin.

It wasn't so much the distance that frightened me, it was more this: he actually *lives* somewhere. He has a life, and I know nothing about it. The concept of occupying a space somewhere, and with it the idea of a home. How a body can belong somewhere; and how you can live in a place and not think of it as home. That perspective, of becoming homeless in that way, being tricked into believing that one thing entails the other, that living somewhere brings about a home. Homelessness is so obviously about something more than just a place to live, and yet the insight hit me hard, like emerging from the backshore in autumn into that sudden vista of sand and ocean, the western sea, *Vesterhavet*, a view stretching out into the infinite, with nothing to see at all to keep you even anchored in the world. The act of walking on that beach, hearing the rush of the sea, the relentless sound of a head banging against a door, abandoned landscapes, abandoned homes, and dogs that slope about and beg at the table of the sky and these empty dwellings.

What did we talk about.

Certainly not our lives, I thought to myself. My mother. Sweden. His music. The fact that my entire family trembled with grief. That my conscience squirmed inside me. That something was always squirming inside me.

The landscape in which we walked; accumulations of black stones, and in between them fierce green moss and grass, sheep shuffling about on legs of reed.

What is it with you and Copenhagen, I asked then.

I can't remember wanting anything revealed, I can't remember wanting to know any truth. But he told me that truth, in a voice that made it seem reasonable to assume it surprised him as much as it did me. This: that he really was someone else's man now, that there was another woman with us on our walk, another woman in bed with us in the afternoon.

He suffered when I touched him.

He suffered when we stood still on the path and looked into each other's eyes; it made us understand what exactly it is we do when we look into the eyes of another. We are two vessels connected in such a way as to divide up the pain in equal shares. Seductive, and yet—in one cynical breath: the same sum, the same amount of pain, only more neatly arranged, perhaps.

I've got a woman there, I live with her when I'm working in Copenhagen.

We bathed from the rocks. We picked our way out into the bay in our ugly footwear, legs bare. I wanted to skinny-dip, but didn't. Both of us were more cautious than is good for bathing in such locations. That was what made it such a lovely scene, I think to myself now. Not removing our footwear, wanting to keep a grip. Not being able to make up our minds as to the safest way of getting to the water. All that hesitation.

It wasn't until evening he asked me the question I've thought about ever since.

Do you think this is dangerous.

Absolutely, I told him. Neither of us knowing if we were supposed to laugh.

The sun was hot, the last warmth of the year. September, the tail end, moreover. The end of season, everything about to board up, ice soon to be packing in the inner waters, at least in theory, in theory and in thought: a winter from which one cannot escape. Snowed in.

We clambered up in silence. I'm not sure I recall, but at some point we went home. I was extinguished like a light, wanting instead to be quenched like thirst. Sadder than ever before or since.

The same night, before we fell asleep, he said something from some drowsy depth, something I have heard him say so many times since, in my kitchen and in my bed, in an airport once:

On that island, walking on that path, all I wanted was to stay there forever.

I think it was the closest we ever got. We stood there for a few minutes, and the island held its breath, everyone else lay with their phones and their rescued marriages, dozing off to sleep. I was the one, this time it was me who went. He came after me. The path was so narrow there was only room for one at a time. I'm not sure I could have done it any other way.

I'm not sure if the new man was aware how sad everything was, the way it all expelled a sigh that afternoon. I don't think he did. We understand each other, only he can't face seeing how unhappy I am. I can't cope with the pain of any more women—right, muso.

And what's with your girlfriend, was something I never asked.

RELAX, EVERYTHING WILL be all right, says the new man. He fiddles with a candle, turning it between his fingers, making sure it's straight, turning it again, another adjustment.

It's under control.

I think about what he means, what exactly is under control. I nod and take his hand, holding it tight on the table between us. He pushes a plate aside, squeezes my hand in a rhythm I fail to recognize from anything in nature.

THE ROOM'S DARKNESS is limp. The night is emptied, its remains deposited in the corners, in her face. She thinks about calming herself with rhymes. She must know so many, how often she must have rattled them off in order to *remain* in a place. She feels an urge to go walking with him. One of their first days together he told her about a hike he had done, somewhere in Sweden, with his mother and his son. How marvelous it had been. That was the word he used: marvelous. I'd like to do it again, he said, and she thought he meant it to be a kind of *invitation*. That it was she he wanted to go hiking with in Sweden. Only it never was.

She extracts herself from his arms, he gives a start, then wakes slowly. She gets out of bed, his eyes latch on to her naked body, then close again. She doesn't think he sees her from behind as she goes to the bathroom to get some water. You can sense things like that. But you can choose to believe he is watching nonetheless.

Maybe he'd rather have been left alone, she thinks. I'm glad you're here, he lies. But she knows: he wasn't watching her, and what he really wants is to be on his own. Like a woman with a little child, who after a while just needs to be *alone*. When at night she begins to dream that not only five infants, but also her man and her parents, her sisters and girlfriends start sucking milk from all her fingers and toes, her nipples and earlobes; when all you really want is to be able to go to the bathroom on your own—and simply be a *self-sufficient human*. If such a thing even exists. I am an instrument of solitude, a tool by which to become myself, to be on my own at last. If this cannot be, she thinks, then I want nothing. It's that simple, too. That there is no reasonableness, but: unreasonable wants, unreasonable love, even when no love exists, unreasonable love is there. What you give and what you get, with no accordance between them. There is something decadent about not loving those who love you. But decadence is only the start. There is something cynical about it. The way there is something cynical about loving a person who has never asked to be loved by you. These are thoughts that may occur to her. A militant, warlike love, boiling away inside her, a subjugation of land. Love resembling violence.

MY DAD WAS suddenly there for me again, her new man says.

They have to duck to walk under the washing on the line. He's got the same pillowcase in his hand as when they started three rows earlier. He keeps stretching it out. She nods.

The enthusiasm in his voice is for this encounter with a father who it seems has never been there for him before, the way no fathers ever are. This, too, is a truth like so many others. Such as them being there always. She bends down and pulls up a top with long straps from the basket. It is entangled in some tights and a pair of his underpants, but he lets her do the unraveling on her own. She wonders if his love for her is actually a love for the space she has cleared inside him. It was like she sorted him out, the way you sort out a basement storage room after a partner has left and gone: shifting boxes and bags, throwing out stuff heavy-handedly and sentimentally at the same time. Until gradually spaces appear, small areas of floor, open, barefooted cubic meters, making room for *something else*. A father, for instance.

HER BODY IS confused, like nature these days; spring flowers finding their way into winter, snow in May, elderflower in February. And now, her childhood lake freezing over, the fish suspended beneath its ice, beneath the glowing orb of a sun. The body is confused, as the air, too, is confused, gusting richly with rented smells of harvest and wool, apples lying stored and silent in barn lofts, rancid fat. One minute her body is a festival, the next it is a darkened tunnel through which passes a shuffling funeral procession. A feeling of *elsewhere*. In the weeks after meeting her new man, she thinks: there is a state worse than wanting something and not knowing what it is. What's worse is: knowing what you want, and knowing it to be found, only not *here*. The mere fact of its existence. Longing is not an emotion, it is a *thing*. It takes residence in the body and has weight. It distorts the face, and you can't sleep properly on account of it being there all the time. An attraction to calamity.

WHEN FINALLY HE falls asleep, he does so on top of her arm. She feels how it tingles and throbs, with no way she can move it. She lies there for hours in that way. Kept from sleep by the fear of waking him. He never asked for me, she thinks to herself; he thinks: I never asked her to come, never asked her to stay. Her new man's breathing is unsettled, fever sweeps through their bed, all is damp. His mouth is open, she sees, it is light enough to see as much. And his feet, sticking out from under the duvet. She thinks: should I ask if he wants a sheet instead. But then she cannot bring herself to utter the words. As if he were a piece of furniture for which there is no longer a use, as if he were dead. She lies there, trapped beneath him, thinking about how she cannot find sleep with her feet sticking out in that same way, a feeling that any part of her not covered by the duvet will be cut away in the night, amputated. Her mother's mother, drawing the cover up over her if she as much as yawned; a child *slept* there, always. Her parents visited her mother's mother and they, too, *slept*. Disasters may be averted in that way. Many catastrophes are mostly about:

being hungry

lacking sleep

believing oneself to be a victim

The victim finds there to be a particular *reasonableness* about everything. After all you've put me through. After all I've done for you.

Her arm tingles; she has never been as comfortable in all her life.

OR ELSE MY mother phones. Mornings are, as ever, a trial. I wake up in a bed without having slept.

My mother tells me things are rough. I sit up in bed and force my legs over the edge.

Things are always rough, I think to myself. She mumbles. My hair is a mess, and the new man reaches out from under the duvet and messes it up even more. I sink my head between my shoulders like a horse about to bite, that expression, ears flat, eyes narrowed like slits of light under creaking doors.

I snap at them.

I'm ill, she says.

I am not breathing. I flex my feet, shuffle further to the edge. You're ill, I repeat, emptied. Those words, and me, emptied.

The new man's hand stops its tousling. I feel the abruptness with which it halts, as if suddenly encountering some sloppy mass on my scalp, something that once had life.

I love you, the new man does not say. I love you, too, I do not reply.

We say goodbye, he has a long journey ahead of him.

He whispers that he is sorry to have to go on such a day.

I know, I say, and know that he is already gone, and I am frightened to death, leaving, in every respect. I should be here for you now.

It's all right, I say. Meaning: it's best this way. Or just: yes.

I'm going to miss you, he says.

I'm going to miss you, I repeat, without lying, for the words are not mine, but his, uttered out of my mouth. One to one, enthusiasm and fear. I have a feeling my body is bad for his. That it pulls him apart, slowly, like an onion, layer by layer. Rotting from the outside, the way onions rot, from the outside. Or from the inside, the way onions rot from the inside. Paler and paler and paler. Younger and younger. The commotion of my affection, loud as bridges. The summer runs like telephone lines through the landscape, his love is unspoiled, for something that does not exist.

My eyes are the only things left in my crumpled face.

BEFORE WE SLEEP we call each other. Our voices are pressed together like teeth in ancient jaws, by time and too little air, in the vicinity of sleep beneath ceilings, sloping walls; he says he's with his parents, that he's so unhappy. I lie a thousand kilometres away from him, albeit in the same room.

The time you have wasted: the time I have wasted, he says, hesitating.

I know that feeling well, I say, believing myself.

We are both adults, though both in the guise of children, the children of parents to whom we have long since become parents. And our bodies are confused: why are we here, in these familiar beds, as they grow smaller and smaller still.

One summer I was so afraid of wasps, he tells me.

A silence ensues. I was lying in my room, he goes on, listening to cassette tapes my girlfriend had made for me.

And all the times I could have gone sailing.

Yes, I say, simply. I don't know how to talk about it.

Silence.

I've no idea where you are, he says eventually, as if suddenly becoming aware that I too exist inside a body. The body of my voice.

I'm in a small room, I tell him. Underneath the roof are two big double beds, two smaller beds, a dresser full of sheets and covers, and a library of books all the way up the wall that is the spine of the house.

I'm in a room like that, too, he says.

It's so incredibly dark here, he says. I mean, really incredibly dark. He talks about the wind, not knowing that an hour ago I sat with my parents, talking about the wind in the exact same way.

Yes, I say, we talk of the wind and it lays down flat, like a dog in the grass. Not wanting to be seen.

I'M COMING WITH you, is all I say. I think it's the best way. For me to make that decision for him. He stands there like a tree.

There's nothing more to think about, I say, tentatively. Only it hasn't even started yet. He hands me the towel, apathetic in all he does. Like the winter, unconsciously repeating itself, a new snow-fall, a new blanket of the same fabric.

All that vanishes comes creeping back.

All that creeps along the walls. That's the kind of winter it was, everything of importance taking place against the walls. All right, he says, if you say so, and gets in the shower as I vacate it. He turns the tap, the water is cold, cold after my cold shower.

I'm not sure, he says, once the temperature is right.

About what, I ask. My voice sounds strange; I am bent double, towelling my hair.

I'm not sure how much time I'll have.

He falls silent, as I have fallen silent.

I have to work, he ventures. Removes his head from the jets of water in order to hear.

I tell myself: he means these coming weeks, this trip; only then I think: that's how it is with him, never really knowing. And then this: that he reckons that's how it has to be, that you have to *know* something.

I think: it's not about knowing, it's about *wanting*. Maybe it's that simple, too.

WILL YOU GO down to the basement with me to find some wine, I ask him. He looks up at me from in front of the bookshelf, on his knees at the CDs. I can go myself, I add, seeing the look of fright on his face. It's just a bit dark, that's all.

He puts his hand to his mouth, his gaze collapses in on itself, his lips close and shrink like cakes in an oven. He trembles, I see that now: you're trembling.

I crouch beside him. What's the matter, I ask, a nervous chuckle escaping on my breath. You don't have to, I say.

He sits down on the floor, head in hands.

I take his hand. I don't understand what's happening, I say.

It's too much for me, I can't deal with it.

It's all right, I say. Really, it's all right.

Everything is so quiet. With my free hand I put a CD in the player and switch it on. There is no explanation, hardly an explanation for anything in this world, I think to myself. There is impenetrability—and there is the world that reveals itself to you in detonations of sound. Nothing in between, neither darkness nor light.

There are images you carry with you all your life. An apple tree bearing its bright red fruit through winter. A bucket reeling beneath a beech tree. A bathroom seen from the floor when you lay there writhing. The window of a greenhouse. And one long attempt to return, to find a home somewhere.

THANKS, I SIGHED, for calling.

You called me.

Yes.

SHE THOUGHT: NOW I will leave this city and never come back. I will leave this unreal night, let it remain in this place, and never return to it. On the ferry she wrote a message to the new man, saying she hoped to see him, that it might be good for them. Your son, she wrote, it would be good for him to get out into the country for a while. Don't think it over too much, she wrote, only to delete it again. She knew he wouldn't come, she knew she shouldn't beg. Like a dog at your legs, she ran like that; unable to find rest anywhere anymore, certainly not in the apartment. Every time he left her apartment it once more became a *desolate* place. It was something he did to it, his way of emptying everything, emptying her.

BUT HE DOESN'T understand I'm using him to postpone death. The way I use everything to postpone death.

I WOULD LIKE to be passed from hand to hand, a warm ring of gold bestowed, dropped between palms. I thought I knew what sleeplessness was; breathlessness, too; I thought I knew the sound of *no plans*. I fall in love with you, and now I discover: I knew nothing of it. There, it's said now. It can be that way sometimes. Now that, too, is a part of my reality.

I rise from the bed in an apartment that still sleeps. You have gone, before the blinds began to wrench themselves free, to hurl themselves against the walls. The apartment, dreaming of waking;

me, dreaming of the apartment's dreams of not waking. I thought we had an agreement that this was different; different from anything leading to rising from a bed in an apartment that never slept, blinds weeping at the walls, and finding a farewell letter you don't really understand. That I do.

My hair, washed, becomes thin rope as it dries.

You balance on the outer edges of your own feet, not knowing if you can avoid the fall, the plunge into your own skin.

Most probably you are boiling in your habitual leather jacket, and most probably you have warmth enough for three.

I don't want to hurt anyone, you say.

And I thought I'd already heard words like that before. But you said them first. I understand you, I say, meaning: I will never understand you.

There is no *one thing* about me that is out of proportion, but my entire body and the rest of the world. You thought maybe my falls were too great, and that nothing within me was of any stable rhythm. And it's true; that, too is true, and all I can say is that the whole world is unstable, the whole world has a pulse, a heart that contracts as the seaweed bladders burst when you walk on the beach at low tide, or as the black seed–pods of the broom rupture in the sun, a hail amid reeds and feather. So much for stable rhythm. So much for proportions.

There is a feeling these days of nature having consumed its stores, the buds are nipped, and we await a flowering all through the summer.

It doesn't mean I don't love you, you whisper, enough breath for only one word at a time.

And no, I think to myself, you're right, I don't suppose it does. But the fact of you telling me this now, as you lie here on top of me, with foraging hands, means simply that you don't love me *enough*.

The love, I write to you on a scrap of paper, the love that does what is right, is the same love that destroys people. There is no easy way, all the good is taken, and we have only remains by which to divert ourselves.

ALL OF A sudden I imagine more seasons. Or one more, at least.

There is a time: for apples that will come when they are but beginnings, the size of little olives, growing on the garden's oldest trees, wild in the woods. There is a time: for apples, growing into sweet fists, red, and sweeter still. There is a time: for apples, letting go, dropping, gathered up, arranged in boxes with newspaper wrapped around. There is a time: for apples, rotting in the snow in the ground in boxes. But where is the season of no apples. The momentary escape from these red eyes. Perhaps they are always here. And then there is no use for seasons, perhaps they do not even exist but in the language. There is so much falling to the ground: rain roofs riders children blood apples ceilings pictures. The summer, melting away before the warmth has come, before summer—what did we have before the summer, something no one cares to gather up or care about. Something you want to swap for something else; something you want to wear out to get to something pure inside; something that looks like bone, that kind of illumination, an island of bone; something like reality, presumably, something that remembers. It might have been snow, or you, you might whisper. But then it's me, whispering, me, calling.

TO BE A *complete* human; only then to be a repeat of another. To remind him of another woman. To be reduced to a symbol. When emaciated dogs are not allowed to be emaciated dogs; when moonless nights are something other than moonless nights. When the past and all one's worries bed down and remain for winter. What kind of autumn then. What kind of winter, what kind of *contract*, the lakes at evening. When encounters can no longer be chance. I wander and search the streets for you. I travel to Berlin to let you find me.

I don't think a person can decide to do anything in this world.

And yet that is what you do. You decide that we cannot see each other anymore. Now I am a symbol of something else. You tell me that. I repeat the words. But what if I am a symbol of everything that is meaningful here in life. I missed you from the very first day, and it has become worse with each day that has passed. Speculation, phone calls, journeys, journeys, seasons, the wish to be a complete human somewhere, a complete season; winter, it could be, winter winter winter.

THE
LANDSCAPE

THE LIGHT IS milk inside the room. I sit up, as well as I can beneath the sloping wall. My nightgown is a rigid tent and belongs to my mother. My legs are stiff, my arms, too. It's the cold. I haven't turned the radiator on. A creak from within my bones, a person can be this cold on a day such as this. It has become winter, and the calender tells me it is no crime, though perhaps it is anyway.

Regardless.

My joints grate like something being extracted from a freezer, my legs shiver as I climb out of the bed. The silence is excessive. It must be late or early, I decide.

The light is alien.

It has been snowing, and what is seen is the brightness of snow, not the light of the sun. I reach to open a window, and imagine my hand going through the pane. The cold is a sharp slap in the face, and my eyes howl.

The silence outside is excessive, and nothing is late or early. That's how nature is, its only utterance: I am here. Reconcile yourself with that.

I lean out of the window and the trees rise up, cold fingers in gloves of white. They stretch away from the ground, but toward what. A sky that is already draped about their ears, heavy with snow.

THE ENTRY CODE is the same, though the lock is new; the smell is the same, and the same sounds on the stairs, the same light. She lets herself in with a code she thought she'd forgotten. It's the afternoon. You're supposed to be here, should we wait until you're here, she texts on her phone, and sends the message to her dead man. She steps inside the storage room in the basement, one light still working. There is a band of narrow windows facing the street. Many of the packing boxes have sunk at one, two, or three corners. There are no vertical lines at all in the room. Everything is crooked, the windows weep in the heat. The air is moist. Passing ankles, and afternoon in the summer outside. Barbeques, a gradual drawing back into the shade. Windows that stick in their frames, blinds pulled down askew. No, he texts back; take what you want. Most of it's yours anyway.

She drops the phone into a pocket of her empty basket bag. A former neighbour crouches down on the flagstones outside, tips her head to speak through the window. The sun slants inside the dimness. Just to think that someone stayed, that someone has lived here ever since. Two years, three almost. The voice of the dead neighbor cuts into her side:

Are you coming back to live, she asks.

No, I don't think so.

She had forgotten about all these things, so much they had accumulated. Plus everything out at the allotment. There are so many *remnants* of them.

These boxes, packed as if for some weekend trip. And all the things she'd forgotten about, and all those she would like to forget in a hurry. And him, texting from Italy. A grief slicing Europe apart. He calls her up, and they're unable to find a way of talking. He lies and says he wishes he could lend a hand, but they both know he is grateful not to be there with her in that crooked room. His relief breaks a hole in the icecap of her loss, is a piece of wood floating in the rainwater receptacle at the side of the house back home. She would expect him not to want to hear about it, that he would prefer to forget; that's the way these things work. But the reality of the matter is he wants to know. About these things of theirs, that are here still. Their having packed away sugar and pasta and tinned tomatoes, spices and wicker chairs, magazines—all with the idea of coming back. The fact that the packing boxes have become damp, that they are disintegrating, that the pipes that run along the ceiling have been dripping, that one drop after another has collected and formed, then to fall; we have awoken in other beds, in other rooms, the fact that she wiped away a bead of perspiration from her brow in a Copenhagen café where her novel is displayed, sadly resplendent in its stand of amber or bone, and the fact that that droplet of moisture penetrated the wall into the basement storage room, there to be sucked up by the thirsty house of cardboard that is sinking around its contents of old photo albums and worn-out shoes, drinking glasses, and vases dulled and fatigued by the biding of time.

She lifts a box down onto the floor, though can hardly find room for it. There is nothing written on it, no indication of what it might contain. She pulls apart the flaps of the lid, and on top are two socks belonging to different pairs. Then piles of American magazines. Some food magazines, and kitchenware. The cast–iron pan they got from her parents for Christmas one time. She runs a finger over its surface and finds it still to be greasy. A drop of moisture descends from the pipe above her head and atomizes against it, myriad beads dissipating across the surface in perplexing patterns. She looks up to see another droplet forming. She thinks of how she oiled the pan with rapeseed oil, only days before they went away. She remembers it always being left out on the stove. Or was that the older one, also from her parents, she wonders, suddenly in doubt. She can't remember. First there was one, then the other. This is going to take months, she thinks to herself.

Later in the evening the light is warmer, an hour comes during which the space is aglow with descending sun, only then to darken almost at once. She is sorting some bowls, thinking about which ones she actually wants. She sighs and sits down against the wall, drinks from her bottle of water. She picks out some cutlery and throws the bluntest knives into a dilapidated box that has quenched its age–long thirst in condensation and become a box for things discarded. The things she knows he doesn't want. In spite of everything. She finds a tablecloth, rolls the good knives up inside it and puts them in her bag. The granite mortar and pestle, too. Some jars of honey, though their contents are mottled with white crystals. Is it yours or mine, that mortar and pestle, she wonders, without knowing for sure. There is a whole case of tumblers, three-sided, flat. Liquor. A small metal sieve for the shaker when pouring, to filter away the flesh of lemon, the seeds, and ice, from the cocktail. Her phone lights up again, and she texts back to cancel a meeting with a friend. She cancels the thought of her dead man even being *capable* of being here in the basement with her. She thinks there would always be some excuse. Some reason for *unfortunately* not being able, no matter he much he really would have liked—and it might be Italy or Copenhagen, work or something else, something getting in the way. You know how it is. She doesn't think it could ever be any different than that. Something like doing something on your own. Like when she used to go for morning walks with him in the woods, the times he tried. He, who had always been, so she thinks now; you, who always will be:

disappointed by the woods.

Everything shifts, the world I describe vanishes word by word, that mother of mine. Everything that has to be sacrificed for something that can never compete with what came first and is most genuine. A lonely place in which to stand, exposed as the trees they allow to remain here and there when harvesting timber, not having the heart in the final analysis to leave the landscape entirely bare. And maybe you come home after a long time away, with a feeling of having been lost—a feeling of why did I go, what was I doing.

The landscape you make your home in childhood is a landscape that forever resides in your face. You carry it with you the rest of the way. And the consternation that awaits: the appalling dismay of returning home. Standing there with a face that doesn't fit; a face fallen, like the trees toppled by wind.

There not even being a home here anymore.

What kind of a face is it that has become,—well, what, exactly. Foreign to the world, planets floating in space, wrong planets, confused, bewildered faces in peculiar orbits around something such as home, something such as an instance of love.

NATURAL DISASTERS DON'T distinguish between what is foreign and what is not. Nothing stays as you left it. The return home is impossible, one must reconcile oneself with a face that is foreign.

The landscape doesn't miss you. The hills have not pined. To the hills, one person is no more or less foreign than another. All people are always both parts: there is always some recognition, something shared; and no one willing to be shunned in that way. Marginalized like foreign bodies, infants mixed up at birth, planets likewise confused. And maybe unreality is like that, too, indifferent as to how much history and how recognizable.

THE THIN MAN'S cigarette divides the darkness in two. He walks along the pavement in the other direction.

The roads go on ahead, they will be home before us, I think to myself.

I have lived nowhere in particular for nearly three years, you confide to the tree, proudly. As though you have wandered without water, now to reap here upon the summit.

There was really nothing I wanted more, you say, halting with your arms slightly extended at your sides. A bit like the crane, its wings out to dry.

Than what, you ask, nothing you wanted more than what; than to show you, I say, to show you how someone lives.

THE DOORBELL RINGS, and she presses the button to open the door without lifting the entryphone to hear who it is; she knows it's him. She adjusts a few small things, places some open books in a pile, lights a candle. Hi, he says. His face is torn open, and expels the image of a person dejected. He asks about her books, how things are going in that respect, and she tells him they're not. Then you must be living a lot, he ventures optimistically.

You could say the opposite.

As if literature had anything to do with any apportionment; anything to do with that kind of fairness. As if fairness even had anything to do with apportionment, balance. She lifts her legs and places her cold feet in his lap. He talks as he rubs warmth into her toes. I've found a new apartment, he says all of a sudden, I'm going to be living on my own. She doesn't entirely believe him, that it could even be possible. He is a ring that passes from one girl's hand to another, is glassy-eyed from encounters of skin. Good, she says. Does it mean you've split up, you living on your own.

I'm not even sure we're together, if you could call it that. She nods.

It's mostly just living together, he says.

She nods again. I'm not sure I understand, she says.

No, he says, I'm not either. The winter is an anesthetic.

But then it's not just the winter.

HE SAYS HE doesn't understand why she doesn't go away for a while. You can write wherever. She turns to the window, tries to push it open, only it sticks.

What's stopping you, he asks. You can make a new home somewhere else.

He doesn't believe it himself. He gives her a hand, a sharp shove against the bottom rail. She imagines his hand going through the pane, a shower of glass descending like a veil, the world outside at once becoming clear, commanding the mind, the way some lithographs do, razor-sharp and in a way more real than anything ever seen. It opens, and the warm air of inside collides with the cold of the courtyard.

Or you could come back.

It's as if he forgets, between each time they speak, that other people exist. That she has someone else, or more precisely, hasn't. That she is tied and bound. That he is.

She looks at him and smiles:

Great, she says, that would be fine.

BABY CARRIAGES IN the courtyard. Windows thrown open, duvets spewed out like foam to dry; the clatter of bicycle locks, back doors that slam, a scattering of green buds, the way nature exists inside the city; an absence of all else but thoughts revolving around *not* revolving around death and winter and men who are no longer here. The impossibility of taking leave of something that never was. Something else that cannot be taken leave of, precisely because it was. Tangibly, when the past is pressed into everything, and when your thoughts are. The fact that there is a storage room in the basement and things there that they have accumulated. An indivisible remainder, everything fractioned, stumps of teeth inside a mouth; she is broken by all their things; she is again broken by the mere thought of what she can remember and what she has already forgotten. That, on its own. When there is no one to witness, a glove in the snow, left behind and forgotten all winter, now suddenly come to light, bulging with something inside, reminiscent of a hand, the humanity of it, dulled suede against the black soil, and then ten days on: snowdrops like stars all around, a sky in the borders, in a corner of the garden.

How many days like this.

How many days of spring can a person actually stand.

THE KEYS OF your apartment were shiny and bright as eyes too old for the face in which they are suspended. The apartment into which you moved that winter when you left me—it was like it was forever uninhabited. From the very start, uninhabited, and it seemed like that would never change. I knew straight away, I . . .

I know I can come here always.

It has nothing to do with will or absence of will:

you never change the lock.

Seen from above we looked like a litter of hungry fox cubs falling over each other in the rush.

Do you love her, I asked you, my eyes darting between new furniture and some things she'd done to dress the place up like a home. A decorated space, and you noticed.

You were sad in a way I recognized from somewhere, though I couldn't gain the purchase to see clearly.

You are quite unable to place something in a room without it looking like it's only temporary.

Do you love her, I asked, and saw the torment come over you, though recognizing it as something unrelated to the wish to escape.

Well, you ventured, hesitating, first man on the ice. No. But I could *begin* to love her. It *could* turn out to be something good.

Do you still love her, the other woman had asked you. And your two replies resounded then together, filling the room from floor to ceiling with dissonant overtones, chain-sawing the air, or anything else that might ever present itself.

Yes. Of course I love her. The way you love a season or a thought. Or: I have loved her. As if the past is past. Blade box: it's easy to leave someone if the swords don't go through the skin, if you can talk about the past as past.

Love someone like a season, a thought.

Both of us then expelling a sigh, thinking: it's already over.

He is no one yet. You are no one yet. And we both of us miss you.

I COME TO your apartment again, out of breath and in a cold sweat. I do not fumble with the keys, I run up the stairs, pull off my jacket and unlock the door in the same movement. I run through the hall, into the living room; throw myself down on the sofa.

Her breathing is noise.

I am not breathing.

SHE ADOPTS HER dead man's sense of the life that is hers not being *her* life, but the recollections of a stranger. An unfamiliar woman's walk down memory lane, everything swollen up, as it were, infected by some nature of explanation and system. The way recollections may be orchestrated to achieve a cohesion that wasn't there before, that doesn't exist in the life that is.

She told him one night as they lay together after strange sex that had seemed mostly like swimming.

His voice was hoarse.

You talk too much, he said.

No, she replied. This is a life lived by another woman, retold by herself.

Who do you tell your life to then, he asked her, and the question sent her reeling. It was the very *reason why* she was lying there, the reason why, in spite of everything, she couldn't be without him in her life, the way he was able to identify the essentials in all things. If ever she lost herself in sentimentality he could pull her from the flames again with only his eyes. To whom do you tell your memories.

His eyes were clear in the dim room.

She said: I don't know. I don't know who I tell. Just someone who'll listen.

Hm, he muttered, on the verge of sleep. Builders would start their work in only a few hours. Their work, patient hammering and the rasp of a saw, became sounds she would later associate with the feeling of being recognized—heard by him, the dead man. Eyes of before.

IT WOULD BE better for you not to live on your own.

I suppose, she concedes, sipping her tea, holding the cup first in one hand, then the other, not wanting to burn her fingers, or for it to get stuck and become a part of her.

You'd have someone to—well, you know . . .

He looks like he's picking a shiny object up off the ground, a coin perhaps, the gleam of a coin:

. . . stop you thinking.

She nods and sips some more tea.

Coming to see her makes him sad, she sees that. It's as if he hopes that one day she will leave with him. As if it would ever be better that way, to have calamity hanging about the place. Circumstances. I'm fine, really, she tells him in a letter after he has gone. There's no reason to be worried, she writes, and says the words out loud to herself:

there is every reason to be worried.

It's to do with other things, that's all. He walks home through the snowfall. It stops around midnight. Snow, piling up in the streets, illuminating the city from below. Street lamps reflecting the snowlight in their copper bellies. Cones of light issuing down through the night, these curtains of darkness that hang draped between the structures of the city. Courtyards silent, as if afraid of being found. No one breathes. Soundless traffic. A hand lit up in the glow of a cigarette.

SHE IS SITTING on the balcony, the one that faces out on the little square and the church. She can touch the plane tree with her foot. In the courtyard are three lemon trees with six lemons between them. Will they stay there long enough to see them ripen. Will they leave before. She waits for him to come back from the grocery store. What was it he needed. Sardines and tomatoes and vodka. The way the house is built is strange. No matter how much she goes about the apartment her body continues to be surprised by the way the rooms collide. Boxes tumble, rooms are kicked into place, and all these balconies hanging from the windows. Could a person live here, is it a home. If you come back, she thinks to herself, then I will stay here forever and will not wait a moment to begin living.

NATURE TOILS AWAY, its eternal seasons; at present I am empty and need someone to pluck up the courage and inhabit regions within me. It's like there are too many plains, and too few animals.
Trees that don't fit in with the landscape here.

Everything happens too fast or too slow. Even nature's rhythm has been nudged awry, even the seasons, and the images hasten away, silent, and yet with disconcerting urgency. Inhumanity all around.

IT IS A dreadful realization: that there is so little one can write about. Practically nothing, and all of it the same. Everything else becomes exotic and, well, irrelevant: unreal. This feeling of unpleasant surprises, from all quarters; one longs for sanctuary and a hot bath, and for someone to have been waiting without having noticed a thing. Either it's knives and scissors, or else nothing is even worth the effort.

The thought that there might be something I perhaps ought to keep from writing, a thought about there having to be something left. Elsewhere.

But then there is no elsewhere.

And then perhaps there is no room for such consideration, maybe it's like that. That all consideration eats you up in the end. I can't even tell a proper bedtime story. Once, maybe, but then they cried, too, and wanted to go home.

There is only one thing to write about: all to which I cannot say goodbye. Including my mother. Including you. My dead man. There is a corpse in the bathroom, I think to myself. There's that corpse I cannot evade; you, and all the love that accumulates.

The images, the five to which I keep returning. The bright apples in the garden in December. They are so real to me. I look out of the window and there is a sense of the world not hanging together. It's as if the winter that is all around the red apples is *arti-ficial*. The apples, however, are so real that if a fire broke out, then the sky behind them, the corner of the ochre-colored outhouse, and the earth beneath them would burn and crumble, whereas the tree would be the only thing left, luminous. A figure, punched out of a sheet of cardboard. One gets the feeling that all reality is only temporary, and the artificial can go on and on. But perhaps with those five images it will be different. In the end. Then perhaps I will be writing not merely to postpone my own death, but to prevent that of the apples. Then perhaps it will be love for you that I demand. A farewell one simultaneously approaches and writes oneself away from.

Bright, shining apples don't know how to cease. They refuse to drop in October, to rot in the grass, and a person cannot forget them in a hurry. Autumn turns into winter, and winter departs to reveal a spring; but the apples know nothing of seasons. They will not accept the haste dictated to them.

I find myself too close to the pane and must wipe away my breath. So cold, the glass—it surprises me. Although it's December, it surprises me. The skin that encloses my body shrinks, an abrupt contraction, a puckering fabric, a curtain *you* draw aside. I step back and sit down on the bed again. Pull my feet up and bury them under the duvet that is still warm and heavy with sleep. My mother speaks out of my mouth: you can't lie there, *lazing*.

What would she know. You can't tell me what to do anymore, I lie.

IT'S LIKE I'VE been running to catch a train, and now the conductor has seen me and waits. What am I waiting for. Me, I suppose. It'll be a long wait, I say to myself out loud. People in the train look at me, a woman squints over the top of her glasses.

I'm tired of waiting.

BUT THERE'S NO gratitude. Just like you can't be, can't continue to be, grateful for being well again after illness, just like you can't be grateful for things not having been worse. Just like you can't find any comfort whatsoever in the assumption that *everything will be all right*.

You'll see.

For the first time during those days, I would not help repair the brickwork, and refused to care about the animals in the stalls. Maintain what.

THE TABLE ON which the candles have burnt out while we slept. Where did the night go. A mess of empty glasses. Even though there are only four in all. A mess. He turns toward the wall, away from the sunlight that fills the room with song. I am up and standing in the middle of the room. Either you'll make a fantastic father, or else you will be no father at all. These are the possibilities for a man like you, I think to myself.

His breathing is unsettled, has no rhythm. Too immersed in

feeling something yourself. A child would release him from the detention of his body. His body, wanting all the time, always in a state of expectation. Something needs to be different, the piano tuner, always a false note in the flesh. Only then it isn't in the flesh at all, it's something else instead, another thirst.

Stay, he says, half in sleep, or else too awake by half.

I stand erect, solitary, a tree where once was forest, a twiggy remnant is how I must look. The light is pale. I shake my head, as though it were neither thought nor reason inside my brain that decided, but a wind sweeping through a landscape. Now that the trees no longer afford shelter, now that I am up.

Awake.

There is always one of us who cannot sleep; in any bed someone must always lie awake. One who cannot sleep a second more. I go about the apartment, gathering things together the way we do in gardens on summer evenings. That same cold feeling of *too late*. One of us is sleeping.

My clothes lie scattered like resting creatures on the floor. I pick them up without a sound, and leave.

You think I'm in the kitchen and mumble my name at the partition. I have closed the front door with the caution of a previous world, ours when we lived in Aarhus. You speak my name more than once.

Dead man, a dead voice, unable to muster the strength to call out.

Unable to summon yourself, you sleep again. You are no one's father, your sleep is your own. Sleep from it all, I think to myself— but sleep sleep sleep, I pray, and descend the stairs on the limpest of legs. It feels like a dam has burst, a gigantic blister ruptured, and now: my body hurtling down through the stairwell. I take with me everything, and leave everything behind. Taking in air only when emerging onto the street. I hurry some ten paces before turning my head back toward the building and casting a glance up at the windows. But you have not risen, you speak to me still through the partition, but it is the brick of the outer wall your voice must penetrate, that, or the window. I creep through the city with eyes closed. To cheat the morning, to postpone something. Already there are dogs. And fresh flowers in the buckets outside the florist's. The air is sharp, the world restless, unwilling to wait any longer. It is quite unsentimental. There are those who come with us, and those who don't.

The city's sky and all the city's streets are the same.

The same brittle light. My relief at having slipped away was the same color as the sky.

YOU'RE NERVOUS AT seeing me. You tremble, I sense.

I thought it would be good for us to see each other, you say, but we both know: it makes no difference if we see each other or not.

A thought such as this: to have to go back and make sure you left nothing behind. To see if you switched off the lights. There is always light left on; always a waste of light in this world.

SHE SURPRISES HIM on the back stairs, wanting to say good-bye. I'm leaving tomorrow and wanted to stop by before not stropping by for a very long time. He flicks the tea towel over his shoulder and leaves it there, shakes the dishwater from his hands. His eyes, scanning the courtyard, trimming everything that is wild. The sun reflects from a metal sheet and some piping left against the wall. Some oak leaves half hidden by snow that will not melt and relinquish itself to any spring. Hi, he says, thinking: what are you doing here. She wonders, and zips down her coveralls, knowing he cannot avoid noticing her blue dress and the necklace.

He takes her by the arm: let me show you my room. She goes inside with him, and there they are; she wriggles out of her coveralls, he wrings his hands and sits down on a chair. She looks around the room and sees her own things. Everything looks foreign in this way, him living here seems improbable, quite as improbable as him not living here. His sentences are short. Small glass prisms dangle from thread in the window. You should see it when the sun comes in, he says, the wall becomes a rainbow. It's like a psychedelic explosion. He throws out his hands. She nods. Places her boots with the heels to the wall. You've got it looking nice, she says, and means it.

Thanks, he says. I should have asked you over before now.

She nods and is glad to be wearing perfume, its scent is heavy now that her body is warm from all her layers of clothes. She feels feminine. He wrings his hands. He is not breathing.

You're pale, she lies. He gives her an apologetic look and then the door opens and his girlfriend is standing there, distraught. You, she says, before correcting herself: hi.

He jumps to his feet, only to stand motionless. Handwringing, teethgrinding, heartrending. I just came to say goodbye, I'll be gone again in a minute.

Okay, she says.

Her mouth hangs open, she is not breathing, it's as if her body is hoping her lungs are as open as her mouth and that the air will somehow find its way in. An icicle succumbing and breaking off, that's how she goes. She leaves a space behind her in the room, like a streak of rust in the picture where she stood. Or perhaps his whole room is a stage, a non-existent place in the world, his life there, for her always: a non-existent life. A plummeting fall that will never reach an end.

It was nice seeing you, he lies.

Was it a bad time, I ask him. He nods: she's thinking of leaving me before I leave her.

Is that what you're going to do.

No, he says, I'm not. At least no more than I always am. It's all like one long attempt to get to somewhere else. That's how it feels. She nods. Yes, she says. That's probably it.

THE SOUND OF grain rushing from the silo; a scraping jaw, ten thousand stones, a sudden descent from on high. The silo is red with rust and there is a smell of cold concrete and hay. The floor is cracked and there's an old Ferguson in the corner. She holds open a sack, and Arne shovels the grain up off the floor. The dust gets in everywhere. The mucous membranes become feeble. A flat paleness all around, a demand for sheen. Winter might just as well come, she thinks to herself. The freedom of driving back through the hills on her own. Settling up in fifty- and hundred-kroner notes. The car heaving itself through the landscape. A feeling of no longer inconveniencing anyone, and yet inconveniencing nonetheless. Shoes on the newspaper in the hall. The rumble of fire in a wood-burning stove, and windows open wide. Are you there. The church bells ringing down the sun too soon. The lawn with its scatterings of stale bread and dismantled chicken carcass. Winter may come now. Winter, too, may come.

IT'S LIGHT ONLY for a few short hours at most in the little attic room of their apartment in Aarhus. They've never got round to putting that lamp up. There's a switch on the wall, to the right of the door, but no cord no socket no bulb. She crouches down and rummages through some boxes with tools in them, and duct tape, until finding a flashlight. She feels like a thief. A beam of light, sweeping faintly over the knots in the timber, a pool of artificial illumination that makes everything different. I must have been mistaken, she thinks to herself. She felt sure the place was tidier, that everything was under control. Only it wasn't. And yet there is an absence of dust. Perhaps the room is too damp for dust. A number of rolled-up posters and some of her sketches protrude from a ceramic pot in a corner—along with your fishing rod, a broom handle, a roll of paper tablecloth. On the wall to the left are some shelves she once put up. Or they did. The shelves aren't straight, they threaten to divest themselves of their jars of jam and chutney, their fruit syrup and shampoo. The packing boxes are on their knees. It was only for a while. The way it always is, with everything: just for the meantime. She manages to place a foot in between a tower of boxes on one side and a basket of workout clothes, she thinks, and his shoes, some volumes of *The New Yorker* on the other. She reaches across some more boxes and opens the skylight. The air is not cool, as she had anticipated. It's as if it refuses to circulate. A jar of preserved lemons. A wicker basket with worn leather banding. An olive tree, a laurel, as if that could survive. All sorts of things that are mine, she thinks. I can't take any of it to Copenhagen with me.

She does anyway.

She could.

THEY LIFT THE table out into the sun at the side of the house.

They have bought smoked mackerel and some tomatoes at the grocery store on the way. Their own tomatoes are still hard and yellow. Or their own tomatoes are just plants with budding flowers. She has painted all the woodwork twice. It shines, black and sated. We must remember to enjoy the first days of spring, she says.

He nods, his mouth full of tacks, because then he is putting new roofing felt on the outhouse where the rain came in, and it is autumn. A few tomatoes remain, dangling like hearts in the greenhouse. The perspiring greenhouse. And chives as well. He fetches salt from the kitchen, and she divides the fish. They sit in the sun. She goes into the outhouse, can hear him working on the roof above her. She positions herself underneath him, closes her eyes, sensing what it's like to have his full weight on top of her. He hammers in the tacks. Dust descends upon her hair, her face.

Would he crush her.

If the roof caved in, would he crush her then.

She looks up through squinting eyes, and sees the gash in the roof. She thinks she catches his eye for the briefest of seconds, then goes outside again. She hands him the hammer he says he needs. Some more tacks. They never mention it, that exchange of glances.

It's obvious he likes to be here, she thinks.

But it's obvious, too, that she is the one who likes to be here. To have him here. With her. The thought of their being here together, with nearly everything they need.

A place that is *ours*.

But only her name on the deeds.

The hoe I leaned up against the trellis, the only sloping angle there is. Everything else is a vertical movement.

His bicycle lies in the gravel in front of the perennials, looking like an animal that has fallen asleep. He looks like one of her very first friends. The sun's a lot warmer now, he says, placing a slice of tomato on a slice of bread. Rather impatient, but *here*, nevertheless.

THEY DON'T WANT to take any more than is absolutely necessary.

She wants to walk all day.

Mist lies between the houses, and the square has been hosed. It'll be hot today, she says. We're going out, what should we see, she asks.

But she goes out alone that day. There's something he needs to do. Some sleep. I sat on the square, he tells her that evening. The life there.

She nods. Some other time, he says. Tomorrow, perhaps. Only then—perhaps not tomorrow at all, she thinks. That, and her feeling that she travels alone, always wishing he were there, that there was something he wanted to do. That they wanted to do something together, movement in the same direction.

HER DEAD MAN wears a long yellow scarf around his neck. He has not shaved, and yet she does not doubt that he has gone to great lengths.

She smiles, walks through the room like a knife cutting its way through the skin of a fish. A grating sheath of scales, at once keenly and with difficulty. He takes pains to smile, to put on a face. They embrace each other, she swiftly withdrawing, almost pushing him away before he falls inside her. She holds up a corner of his scarf: nice scarf, she says. He bends his neck to look at it. How hard it is for him. Being here.

You came early, she says.

He nods. He is a child leaving home every day, or: he is the tide, returning and retreating. By turn obstinate and governed by something outside himself, something inside himself—but then perhaps all of life is like that; an eternal state of arrival and departure in a pattern over which one has no control; a rhythm one must simply tolerate.

She wishes the new man had not been with her today. It is as if he now is reaping all that was sown before. Me, she thinks.

He has nothing to give to her, of this she is constantly aware; there is nothing like a ripe time. That time was long before; it's always difficult, a continuing state of exception.

Already everything is too late.

When did that happen.

Her dead man—the look in his eyes, effortlessly sweeping all the flowers and all the wine and all the piles of books from the table.

So much parting collected in one room.

This is your day, someone says to her. Her stomach tightens into a knot. She cannot remove from her mind the thought that someone else knitted that scarf for him; and that the new man has never been as unhappy in all his life. Displaced, in every respect.

Her dead man has brought an old friend with him, understanding nothing. Or perhaps he cannot bear to recognize himself in this room. He is holding a bottle of champagne. It's for her: this is for you, he says. As if champagne were the solution to a puzzle. And then they leave, the two of them together, to be there no more. No longer to be present.

She drinks a glass of white wine rather quickly, and is introduced to a man with a Russian name. His lips promise, but cannot be pictured again; he is there as one looks at him, only then to be gone; broken faces embed themselves within you; whole faces are forgotten.

Because they have yet to reveal themselves in pieces.

All that has not revealed itself to be *art*.

I COULD STAY here forever, he says. But what he means is, he would like to have a home. The night is warm. The sun goes down between the houses, and all the roofs look like they're painted on. Thrusting surfaces of earthen red and ochre. They have only the shoes on their feet.

Their backpacks put next to each other against the wall.

It is cooler inside the room than out. One night in every town, that is their rule. And no more than three days planned ahead. Always they are dashing for trains. Always they come from something better, and always on their way to somewhere supposed to be fantastic. They sip coffee at a railway station café, tucked into a booth with a bench upholstered in red leather. It sticks to the thighs. A dog goes by, dragging its leash behind it. A voice on the loudspeaker announces another change of track: *binario due, binario cinque, binario due,* and the train is continually late. Ten minutes, twenty minutes at a time. We could have had lunch, he says. She nods; they notice a supermarket that will be cheaper. A deserted beach that turns out not to be deserted at all, though for a short while it is. It's like the book she's reading is better for being read here. Or different, at least.

She is disappointed by Pompeii, but decides not to mention it. She thinks there is more Pompeii to be seen in Berlin, that the whole world is spread out over the whole world. Italy in Berlin. Egypt in Berlin. Berlin in the USA. The USA in France. She places a sheet between her thighs. The heat is tremendous. She wakes up early. The sound of a truck braking. A clattering in the back yard, the sound of a metal bucket overturned. A thirst for water. She gets up and has a shower, lies down beside him again in a single movement. She draws something through the room.

I'M AFRAID I'VE forgotten everything. I have forgotten the first time I saw you, and I have forgotten how we got from the *højskole* to your parents' summer house. I can't remember seeing your parents for the first time. I can't remember what it's like to wake up with you. I can't remember what it feels like to come home to an apartment shared with someone else. With you. An apartment that is another person's home. I can't remember what it's like to be so close to another person, almost merged into one; I simply can't remember that I could look across at the door and that you would push it shut with your foot, because you were nearest. I can't remember my annoyance at watching you be so slow and meticulous. With breakfast. With envelopes. I can't remember my anger at finding you passed out on the sofa. Again. I can only remember finding you like that. I can only remember that you were slow and meticulous. I can remember your parents. The feeling of everything being *the first time.* The summer house I remember, but the days spent with you there I have forgotten; the shrubs of broom, your mother pruning them with a pair of shears. You whispering to me not to tell her they should be dug up instead, that pruning them was a waste of time. And the plantation of trees, the short cut down to the meadow. I have forgotten how far the meadow was. And the feeling of waking up rested and refreshed, though with an aching head from having slept up against you, that too I have forgotten, the way it felt; and now I can't understand how that could be, with you now lying here again, so close to me that my body is an extension of yours. With so much still *missing.* With so much being something else, and you still existing.

THE DUST OF the grain, drifting in the sun, vanishing in the shade.

Summer.

The leaseholder passes through the stable. He is visible and then not, in the light and in the dark. He walks as though keeping time to a ticking watch. Each entry into darkness causes all sound inside the stable to be consumed.

But then he becomes visible in the darkness, and quite transparent in the sunlight. A new order. And the shiny ribbon of the feeding trough on each side of the aisle, licked clean and worn down over the years by rasping tongues.

The door is dragged aside with a clatter, sun streams in, the floor ablaze in its light, made to flame by the legs of the cattle causing shadows to leap out across the concrete in panic. Three at a time, the beasts jostle their way down the aisle, haunches taut, skin draped over bony spines; the heavy sway of udders. Their legs can break. Cows are always too heavy for themselves. The nervous way they proceed, neither walking nor running—and never anything other than eager. Never anything other than uneager. It's as if there's something they have to get done before anyone finds out. And like a fan, this tide of cattle spreads and unfolds. All that body falling into place. They are cast in the concrete. Each cow knowing its place, a bit like waves on the shore, their movements a matter of course, a routine, something reminiscent of nature.

She keeps thinking she sees him coming, that he's changed his mind. A friend calls and apologizes. Not so much on his own behalf as love's. It being the way it is, without justice. Justice has nothing to do with love. Justice has to do with business, money.

Fortunately time helps, she lies.

It doesn't, is all he says. Most likely it will always be with you; bear that in mind.

You're right, most likely it will, she says. I suppose you know what you're talking about. Someone has left something behind inside him. No coming of spring can ever make amends. The cows that emerge first spill out through the doors, over the yard and across the road. Stiff legs verge on breaking into a thousand pieces, clouds of bonemeal under their bellies; the field, soft, sprouting its grass. What is it for. And to think one day you would sit here again, on the ground, where the stable used to be. An empty space now, with the sky falling down upon it. The cows don't pay their way. Do I, she wonders. She calls him in Copenhagen. She gets back on her feet and walks through the city, and he lingers on every corner. While another lingers in her thoughts. And in his. And she finds herself thinking there will be more and more threads, they will be shorter and shorter, and unable to join up. And more long sentences discovered to be false. More short ones making sense.

Come, the leaseholder shouts, dragging the sliding door aside.

Come, she tells him on the phone. But he must stay in Copenhagen, he is needed at work; and his new girlfriend isn't happy about us seeing each other, he says. About you not letting go, but otherwise I would, and so on.

A time, inhabiting the body.

A time for that, and a time for something else. A troubled month, or just a troubled night. A magnetic night. An overfilled bed, alone. So now this is where you are once more. And the ribbons of snow are the fan the cows were then; tight French braids, some voices, at least three, weaving in and out; sentences becoming shorter and shorter.

THERE IS A sunrise, occupying a stretch of time. Light, softening the horizon. Doing something to sound.

Branches, graphic silhouettes.

A sky, becoming a sky. Someone loses a shoe on the pavement, a shoe picked up and handed back.

Sit still.

I win a prize for having written something down in order not to forget what it was.

I win a prize and am resigned to the fact that you will never be interested in me. I am resigned to the fact that you will never be anything but interested in me.

The branches are black already, but the light against which they are seen makes it more apparent. That I have woken up too early and am standing here in my parents' house, watching a sunrise as it mimes a sunrise past.

Aarhus Bay: a morning there.

The skerries, Sankt Anna Skärgård: a morning there.

I do not miss you, for I have yet to understand that you are there to miss. In other words: that you are not here. And now, again, the branches, cutting up the picture. A light that spills into the sky from below. A tea bag, seeping into a napkin.

Humility in the face of the kind of order for which one is no match. The thought that all this is temporary. The stables are temporary. My mother is temporary. Us living together during that period of time, and you beginning to doubt. You speaking the words out loud, without intending to. My life, forever in flux. An image segueing into another. A permanent state of transition—only a transition. The fact of insisting on something until one becomes ready to insist on something else. The tulips looking like they've come from a shop, when you don't have me to arrange them.

You are waiting for things to be different. You are waiting for this transition to be complete, of you *learning to live in a place.*

I can see, the way things are, that you cannot come. Because you are already here.

Or because you would want to stay.

BENEATH THE WINTER lies a wandering across the field. A walk through tall grass. Sandals, bare legs, dry meadow grass swept apart, to bow and break, and flatten like a tongue fallen out in my wake. A fleeting heel becomes an image trampled underfoot. Yellow cudweed, an island. And then: grass again, and self-seeded fir, hardly more than twigs, sticking out of the ground. That's what they look like. But then this was before, I am ten years old and we have leased the land from the state. It's August, and I don't know if the willowherb can bloom at this time of year, but I remember the willowherb in flower, a curtain of troubled purple, strangling the brambles. That way round: the flowers strangling the brambles, and then in another image the brambles alone, blue fingers and red plastic bowls. It's like the willowherb's purple is the same as the fingers', like the juice of the brambles reveals itself to be flowers, like the flowers have been pressed together into hard pellets, these berries, now ripe and sweet, and which too, well, reveal themselves. Eight kilos. And just as much sugar. And many more jars, and all the steam running down the windows. We see feet being lifted and placed in front of legs, and the grass as it bends and yeilds in front of us. Bare legs so briefly concealed from view, appearing again.

Walking across the field today, the creaking snow, walking there in summer. Yours being the eyes that see the soles of my feet. The landscape actually being you. You lying in a bed in Copenhagen, it being evening, and you lifting her hand from your chest once she has fallen asleep. Or just the thought of it. Or the thought of her walking through the same grass. Or turning round to see that no one has been there. I turn and look back. Between the woods and me lies the indiscreet snow, disclosing my path, disclosing something more besides. I don't quite know *what*. You, perhaps. It could be you.

THE DAY DRAGS on. My mother sits down at a table, it's mid-afternoon. Always some stack she needs to get through. That's how it is with her, she works her way through her stacks, which grow while she sleeps, whenever she looks away. She monitors them well, but it's no use.

Everyone must sleep, once in a while.

It'll soon be dark, she says to me, meaning she wants me to go. I look up from my book, lifting one leg to gauge how tired they are. When you sit still you lose touch with your body. A humming noise comes from somewhere. I think about what it means to have grown up in a house ever pervaded by the sound of a clock. If it can make you ill. The church bells, ringing the sun up and down. If that's why you move away. And because the thought never occurs to you that the sound might be stopped by means of some simple action. An electricity cable, who knows. I think to myself that the humming noise is perhaps simply the sound of a home, more like the sound of sand running away than that of the hands of a clock, fingers flicking through newspaper piles, the rustle of a bag of dry cat food, more the sound of a straw bale being dumped from a great height onto a concrete floor. A door opening, then closing again. And this continued movement is a counting down, that much home. So high up, and so close as hardly to be seen, hardly to be heard. For it has entered your flesh and being, and *is* now, simply, your eyes; to find that secret place where the mottled hen has begun to lay its eggs, to break those eggs into a bowl, to nudge aside such an angry fowl, or to have my mother do so instead. With big gloves on.

And the knowledge that these movements are a counting down and not a counting up, and that you will need to remove yourself from all of it.

One must establish a state of homelessness within the home in order to make room for oneself. And the eyes and the eggs and the brambles are there, and the sound of pellets of dry food clattering into metal bowls like a hail of buckshot, a shortness of breath.

My legs are no more tired than usual. They are always tired. If you pause to sense how they feel, then I suppose that's how they are. I stretch myself, the soles of my feet bracing against the armrest of the sofa. I relax, and the cat mimics my movement. Do you want out, I ask her, and she lifts her head, peers out at the snow falling—and simply sees. But she cannot, for she has always something else to be getting on with. Before she can eat, before she can sleep, before she can pause to *sense how she feels*. There is no room for her in such a life. And yet there is nothing else.

Room.

The cold light as it issues from the snow, all its whiteness, the winter tore at her face, a tinkling in the living room, like shattered

ice in the swell, beneath a sun as pale as this. The crystal chande-
lier, hanging so still above the dining table, folders and documents
strewn about like skinned animals, ring binders with gleaming
metal ribs, a slaughterhouse with meat hooks that dangle from
above, along the length of the ceiling, the page and the poem I have
copied down. That's how it feels sometimes: that creative writing
has nothing to do with it. You copy down what is. There's nothing
mysterious about it, not a penny's worth of imagination involved.
The object is to become anaesthetized in order that one may be
thriftless with the self, to see without the, well, what, exactly. Illu-
sions. Stories. A wish to see the world as it is, here and now. Perhaps
most of all to muster the courage to desist from creating narratives.

When all sentences are hooks by which to barb the world. A
pyre of nostalgia; when a home is a state of affairs, and you know
it. Reconciliation with the transience of all things, the return home
that resides in that. A realisation of flight, to flee, and escape being
the only place in which to be; in all that is temporary, the only
place upon which to stand. The only place that is stable and will
not sink; an insistence on there being, for every locus of predica-
tion, every flag of adornment, a sentence that hasn't the strength
to keep up the pretence, the vanity; it's like nature taking over, a
birth, perhaps, is what it most resembles. How can a woman scream
in such a way, how can anyone write something as *hard*.

But maybe that's the only thing you can do, when all else is:
pulling the wool over one's eyes, talking down to the world, talking down to you.

How can a person speak that way, so cynically. But then it's
anything but cynical, anything but exactly that: cynical. Maybe
it's the only thing you can do. An open mind, advancing into the

world. Either by paring away or else the opposite, by sewing the world together in patterns new and surprising; memory, conception, perception, reflection. Two movements the same; a desire to be able to see, and to say what there is.

Perhaps it's the only thing I can say: I love you. Nothing else but that. I don't love you. Sentences like that are only true for a moment, uttered in a certain place. From here, this is true.

A person speaking in love is the most touching of all things, if one is able. To accommodate. To sense the person within the words.

My mother cannot go outside with me, her body convinces her a person can conclude a matter, that one's life can be orchestrated in that way. She breathes deeply, a sigh of sorts, meaning no. As if I could have imagined differently, but this is my gift: to allow her to wince. In this way, my mother is forever a child overlooked. In this way, I love her. I must. The way it is choreographed in the spine. Someone has to do it the whole time, love her; maybe that's a preposterous thought, but it's the way I feel about it: that she deserves a constancy of love. And my father: what about my father. Where is he.

I pull an orange knit-hat down onto my head and go out through the mudroom. Before the door even shuts I hear my mother call out behind me, asking me to feed the birds. I'm dressed for it now. I take the trash out with me and untie the knot of the bag. The garbage men haven't been all week, they can't get through the snow. Three full sacks up against the wall. I press the trash down slowly, not quite knowing if it's because I'm scared there'll be some broken glass; only I find myself thinking about some nice drinking glasses I once saw. Mouth-blown, I think, though I don't remember where. They had a kind of knot halfway up the stem, like a knee. I wanted to have some, the glass was green, and even if you never saw them before you would *recognize* them when you did.

The snow goes on. In Copenhagen, a thought to which I keep returning, in the cities of Paris, Vienna, rain and snow that cannot escape. There is no room. Water rises in the streets, snow compacts, layer upon layer. Advancing up the walls of the buildings, consuming floor upon floor. No one can breathe. Towers protrude, steeples. And children standing on top, with foxes on leashes. That image—the way they drink their tea or warm milk, expelling pillars of steam from their nostrils as they sit upon the tails of rooftop weather-cocks, attic-room apexes, sharing an orange in equal parts beneath the sky.

I don't know what it is about disasters that is so appealing.

That is what I want. To sit there. Or lie there, buried alive. Windows shattering, one by one. Water gushing in, the way horses fill a stable. A frenzied struggle for life, and what rules may exist by which to win. A matter of he who has the most wins, I think to myself, and lift the lid of one of the two blue barrels of grain, shovel wheat and sunflower seeds into a bucket. Every seed and every grain, for the birds are waiting in the branches of the trees, and the garden has eight feeding stations. Eight is always the number. Eight paces between the feed store and the manger in the stable. Some things match up that way.

We're at your grandmother's, my mother tells me over the phone, a month after we buried her.

How long does a place go on belonging to a person.

Does a grandmother cease to exist only when the heirlooms have been allocated.

What does it mean, my returning home to a village where the leaseholder has pulled down the rectory stables.

I replace the little roof of the birdhouse outside the kitchen window, and a moldered piece of cardboard drops out and lands in the snow. I pick it up and hold it between my lips as I put the roof back into place, then stuff it into my pocket. Everything is turning into something else all the time. I don't miss you anymore, have never missed you. I empty the bucket, upending it and striking it four times with the shovel. The snow contains a firmament in reverse. Dark spangles in the white. The footprints of a bird are another alteration of the picture. All the time, the landscape is new. All the time, there is something else one remembers. All that comes, and all that is lost. I have a feeling of homsesickness, but perhaps it's not that at all. Perhaps it's the opposite, a disconcerting sense of inversion. That my homesickness is actually a home, this magnetism a feeling of *too much* home, a face revealing *too much* belonging, a flailing, headlong plunge into a landscape in which to become. Become what, exactly. Invisible. Or simply oneself. *Here.*

THE LANDSCAPE HAS torn itself away. Its constituent parts are in motion or else still and separate. The hill extends from the rhododendrons on the eastern side of the house to beyond the washing line and the oak trees along the boundary. A single sweep of slope. The field on the other side of the boundary, where the snow lies in elongated drifts, is another. A bonfire one summer, that you later understand to be a person. Laughter at the fact that you can spend your time eternalizing one thing and another. Art. Theatre, a conquest of land. And a feeling nonetheless of having a responsibility. They are removing soil from mushrooms with toothbrushes.

She wonders if he can remember once having said to her that she had grown so thin, that her head seemed too big for her body. That she looked like an *African*.

She recalls the way she squirmed in the passenger seat. It was hot, and the sun slanted into the car. The next time they stopped for gas, she ran into the restroom to look.

She always focused on appearing to eat more than she did: I *eat*. She placed a bucket of cold water outside on the veranda in the shade. When they carried the things in from the car and unpacked, she put a carton of milk and a bag of frozen peas in the bucket and pushed it under the bench out of the sun.

They drank fizzy drinks together outside, until the mosquitoes came and chased them in again. They woke up too early, or else they woke up all the time, never finding sleep; the place kept waking them up. If I was on my own here, she said to him in the night, I'd be miserable.

So what are you now. Now that you're here with me.

She decided not to cry any more that night.

He slept.

Are you asleep.

I won't fall asleep until morning, she remembers thinking to herself. The place kept getting in through the tiny windows, insistent. And she didn't sleep: at 6 A.M. she began to fondle his earlobe, blowing gently into his ear. His hand swatted out in sleep a couple of times before his body submitted and his eyes opened. Where have you been, she wondered, what dreams have you dreamt, she said. Mm, he said.

She goes out onto the veranda and retrieves the carton of milk from the bucket. He comes out in his underpants and a sweater, wooden shoes on his feet, a bag of oats in one hand, a packet of raisins in the other. This is how they seat themselves on the bench. The milk carton drips onto the decking, then stands in its own pool on the table. It's cold enough, he says, meticulously pouring a measured amount onto his oats. He eats like a ritual, sleeps in the same way. A change has taken place: what began as a singular exception has become a state of exception; which in turn has become a state of repetition, that has become an instance of love. Exception has become ritual, and the ritual is now quotidian. Love has become a ritual. Sex has become a ritual. What are we going to do today, he says. She thinks: survive. I was thinking of going kayaking, he says. Or maybe we could go fishing.

Some time passes.

Maybe, he repeats with a nod. Coffee.

We'll need to get the stove going, fetch some wood, and that.

Yes, you're right, he says. The wilds of Sweden, I'd nearly forgotten.

The wilds of Sweden, yes.

He slaps his arm. Mosquito, he says. She laughs.

The wilds of Sweden, she repeats.

And you didn't sleep a wink.

No, she says. You could say that. They laugh, and their laughter is recognizable from somewhere. From where, exactly, she doesn't know, but recognizable, nonetheless.

ALL KINDS OF things we said to each other that had already been said. I read out loud from a manuscript, and you listened, shifting uneasily. I have begun to doubt whether you actually understood that I was *real*. That I was *there*.

I get the feeling I could become someone else. If I pulled myself together.

But then it's your feeling instead.

You shiver in the sunshine on the shore. I pull a blanket up over our legs, lie down on my stomach again, flick back a few pages in Duras's *Moderato Cantibile*. Start from there again. So now we are lying here. What is it that keeps postponing reality. That's my feeling.

Expectation and postponement, and nothing else.

SHE PHONES TO cancel an appointment. What excuses might be valid. The body does not count. The weather does not count. Disasters count.

IT'S SPRING ALREADY in Berlin, her father writes. It's just the place to be.

She writes back and says it's nice to know that spring is on its way. That it's nice to know they're thinking about her, and that she is thinking, too—I'm thinking about you, too, a lot.

The confusions are many. Sentences begin to doubt themselves. Mothers suspect they are less woman than other women, less mother.

A bit like me, she thinks.

A couple wrap themselves around each other and kiss, and think everything is for *the first time*. Roasted chestnuts, for goodness sake.

ARE YOU COLD. They arrive back at the hotel, and he has been drinking. She pulls her legs up underneath her on the sofa and puts her head in his lap. Warmth, and the feeling of having a home in the midst of *being away*. I'm tired, she says. He mutters something back. Smooths his hand across her hair. Nudges her playfully. Be still, she whispers. Leave me alone, she thinks. He reaches for the remote and changes the channel. She closes her eyes; I don't understand how you can be tired now, he says. He shifts her body, altering its position; placing it so as to give him room. She is so tired of wanting to be somewhere else all the time; it's mostly that kind of fatigue that consumes her. And the next day there is a bird sitting on the railing on the decking outside. He wants to stay asleep. She lies there looking at the bird. She does not rise. It hops about on the railing. Flits down onto the ground, hops about there, as if searching for something. Other places. He doesn't understand that a person can long to be home when they have no home to long for. I am here, what more do you want. That was what he said. Wasn't that what he said. Quite without irony. But there is no logic in the world. Who told you that. That there is a *logic of dreams*. Whatever it might be. There is *awake*, and there is *asleep*, and neither of the two states cause the world to work by any principle of logic.

She is tired all the time.

She is awake again, she can never wake. No two things exist in this world that may be kept apart, she thinks. She gets up, her legs are stiff and sore from all her odd positions. She slides the glass door aside, so the place may enter. She lies down cautiously again. The bird wants in, but hesitates. It is transparent. One understands in some way what it is frightened of.

THEY LIVE IN the last apartment block before the woods, where the detached houses begin. Do you remember the first time we saw each other, he asks.

He beams.

Yes, she lies.

They are watching a French film that takes place in cold rooms. Beautiful women with dark hair. Water. You don't need to know anymore. More doesn't interest her.

But you remember it best, she says, staring into the blue rooms.

They live in the last block, before the city ends.

All their furniture is hers. She remembers the first time she thought: if I leave him all he will have is an empty shell. He owns nothing except the apartment.

The three actors kiss. All conceivable combinations are enacted. Albeit simply.

They go to a bar and eat nuts. As if nuts were a solution to anything. They drink themselves senseless, and full of life. So potentially lethal is how they understand themselves, that much is obvious, as if everything were a frenzied blur, only then it is the exact opposite. Immaterial.

Do you want some tea, she asks.

No, he replies, without considering.

Do you want some wine, she asks.

No, he replies. I don't drink anymore, you know that. I've given it up.

She gives a shrug, her skin is a stiff coat. She sighs and leans back in the armchair. She reaches to the shelf behind her, removes the cork from an already opened bottle with her teeth. Spits it into her lap. She pours some port wine into his empty water glass and uses that.

YOU LOOK TIRED, my mother says as we finish the game. I tell her I'm pale because it's winter. This is how I look when I have no makeup on. In winter. Are you sleeping well, she ventures, tipping the green marbles back in the box. They sound like cattle crossing a concrete floor. A downpour of hooves. A sense of many restless movements coming together in a sudden fever of activity. Earth trampled into mud, a concrete floor, foaming with sound. A cauldron of hooves, boiling over. I look out of the window behind her. The view of Lene and Henrik's apple orchard, behind their house. As if it has never been disturbed.

Is it three years now, I ask.

Since what.

Since Lene died.

Yes, my mother says, too quickly. I look at her. She looks away. She sweeps my own marbles across the board, collecting them in the corner for red, unaware that she is trying not to think about her illness. It is something she does without volition, like a function of the body. She is enveloped by warmth, her cheeks flush, abruptly, as if suddenly she has caught fire. Reaching for the lid, she knocks over my cup. A tongue of tepid tea unfurls upon the table. We sit quite still and stare: it inches toward the edge. It trickles, and drips without sound. Tea soaking into the carpet. Calmly, I pick up the cup and get up to fetch a cloth. I shuffle, to keep the throw around my legs.

I return, and my mother has not moved, not even her eyes. Her gaze is tethered by the little pool that has appeared on the table. The ceiling light reflects in it, but my mother's gaze seems fixed on something beyond, beneath the tongue, beneath the pool. A wet table. I lay a dry tea towel on top, and my mother gives a start. She has left her eyes behind, I catch myself thinking.

How clumsy of me, she says. Anyone would think it was me who couldn't sleep.

You're not alone, I think to myself. Such sleeplessness does not make you pale and fatigued. As long as one of us is sleeping, and there is always one of us who can, and one who cannot.

She puts the lid back on the box, and I feel the waft of air pass across my hand as she presses it into place.

How's Henrik coping. On his own, I ask.

How does anyone, she says, as if to win time. He's working again, at least.

I nod. As if that were any indication. She reads something out. Knowing I already know and couldn't care less.

I think it's tearing him apart, though, she says, and looks up at me. Her not being here anymore. It's strange, isn't it, that we survive each other like that. The way people go on living in the objects they leave behind. Things become so oddly meaningful. A wheelbarrow in a garden, a basket left under an ash tree.

She shakes her head.

You're recovered, I say. Your treatment's finished now.

Yes, she says, and thinks me wiser than that. For it has only just begun, and will never be any different. One does not simply put aside a grief of such nature, it cannot be talked into submission, nor be vanquished by any conspiracy of silence. It's like it is with you, like with all things momentous. They come back at you in a loop, and with increasingly greater force they kick the air from your lungs.

I have a short list. The older I get the longer the list will become. You are on it. My mother is on it. The kind of days when you realize things will never be any different, that you have lost, lost, lost. When that is the way it sounds: three or four times in a row. Such a blow to the gut: you.

Of course he misses her, he's bound to.

Of course, I repeat. I'll go up and see if I can sleep, I lie. My mother has turned in her chair, is looking across at Lene and Henrik's house, where an upstairs light is on. One only, upstairs.

Alright, she says.

Alright, she says again, and turns toward me. Good idea. Take the throw with you.

A
FUNERAL

WE WERE TOGETHER. That was how I worded it. When I tell others about it, that's what I say. We were together. Whatever that means. Whatever it might involve. A fear inside me that can be kept at bay like that, but then again. It changes nothing, one could just as well say the opposite about us. That we were never together. We lived together for a certain number of weeks, a certain number of months and days. So what happened, one might ask. What happened then was that we were no longer together. Perhaps the truth is simply that, that it will never be more complicated, always that simple: that you are together, or else you are not. It is not a matter of decisions and emotions, or anything in the way of agreement. It is the body that continues to have the final word. The tangibility of where you're at in the world. Whether you are in a room together, or not in that room together. Our bodies make the arrangements, brains do nothing. The manager of the ice-cream kiosk at Svinkløv Badehotel, where I once had a holiday job, told me one afternoon when the rain was keeping everyone indoors that ninety percent of what we communicate is communicated by the body. But it's not true. I know that now. Everything is told by the body. Our thoughts and words are all tied up in the body, in the lips, in the hands that tremble or lie still in the lap, when for instance there is nothing more to reach out for. All is movement or absence of movement. Something plummeting. Something else wandering across a landscape. A body wandering across a land-scape, a thinking body, a living human being. As long as it lasts: life. One can miss a person, love someone, and yet leave them.

And this, too—the insistence on being concerned, though not nostalgic. The insistence on grief, and on remaining within it.

The insistence on possessing a body, quite simply that. Nostalgia purges the body, nostalgia steps inside one's thoughts like a mali-cious guest, a sudden urge to frighten your sister—did you know you were adopted, that they didn't want to tell you in case having no parents made you sad. Hateful incisions that force one to keep a cold compress—the fabric of one's dress—in place over the flesh. And then the correction of that same urge. There is no momentum in nostalgia, one is unperturbed, having circumvented the body and the concern that is attached to having a body, to moving for-ward in time, forward across a landscape. Can a landscape termi-nate—can one go to the edge, step forward and fall; the collapse of a building, a cliff, animals. And the woods, they too, a downpour of rain, ironed clothing on hangers, the kind of day when it takes more than just that.

To enter inside the grief and remain there. One might think that the backward step into the nostalgic is a harmless one, and for that reason that one can only be free of distress, without body. And yet I cannot think of anything more perturbing. To walk backward over the edge, divested of one's body, to plummet without, and die as such bodiless. I will insist on being a distressed person within the world, continually coaxing nostalgia into my being, the struggle that is. To proceed backward and forward at the same time. Nostalgia comes of a fear of death, of simply not living enough, possessing emotions of sufficient depth. I wish only to try and see the emotions that are there; to remain in grief, and go back only in order to be here. Inside my own body, a ghastly face.

I DON'T GET it, he says. I mean, if you still don't want me.

Are you having second thoughts, she asks.

I've *always* had second thoughts, he says; I never left you.

Okay, she says, picking up her bag from beside her chair. She thinks about her, whether he is seeing her now, or if it was just fascination, the way he said.

Okay, he says, acquiescing, collecting himself like a shattered glass, walking through the city in that way. Picking up shards as he goes, dripping through the streets, gashing himself relentlessly.

She thinks to herself that it is perhaps not a fascination with another person, more a dream of something else, *something* existing that can do that to a person, render one's body *free of distress*. That such a wish can destroy so much.

She loves him more than ever before, slowly relinquishing their being together.

SAY SOMETHING, TELL me something, he says.

Have you seen the snowdrops over there, she says, with a nod toward the trees in the park.

And there, in the flowerbeds, he says. So many signs of spring now, you dream of them at night and in the day they make you ill. She nods. She understands what he's talking about.

And in summer it's the heat, she says.

You dream of it at night . . .

. . . and in the day it makes you ill, he joins in.

Exactly.

She asks him: Do you know that feeling . . . like there's a predominance of things you *remember* that will hardly leave you alone. In the spring. Because it reminds you of so many things. Other springs. Other people you used to love, she thinks to herself, he thinks to himself.

He looks at her and she cannot gauge the look in his eyes, cannot tell if he is angry or impassive. And then she knows what it is. A spectrum of colors contracting into a beam of cold light. A look that could cut glass.

Yes, he says, inquiringly. Is it something you want to talk about. Is that what you want. Is that really what you want. That's what he thinks, she knows he does.

She lowers her gaze. They are seated on a damp bench, her skirt is wet, her jacket, unlike his coat, not long enough to protect her thighs. She sits there, and tells him too much. The jealousy, what it does to her.

What is it you miss, she asks herself. Seated there, four, maybe five useless thoughts in her head. I was never even happy when we were together. What's different now. Everything's the same, only worse. Because both of them are older now; we are older now. It only makes things worse to have grown older and wiser and still be making the same mistakes. The dawning realization that it will never be any different.

He gets to his feet, scuffs at the ground. She wants to go back to the apartment. I'm going home, we can talk another day.

I OFTEN HAVE such thoughts, of being able to go home. Snow has fallen again. Not much, but all the windows are edged in white, the rooftops upholstered. That kind of wrapping up of bodies and objects. I have no desk at which to work, still no desk. I think it might make a difference. If I had a desk to work at. Then I could get to my feet and leave it, on a Friday afternoon, for instance. Today, I could get to my feet and let the books be a job. Go home to something else. To something *other*.

Whatever that would be.

I feel guilty about not having a proper job, but every time I try one, every time I have a job, all I can think about is going home.

A proper education. A proper person. As if some people are more *legitimate* than others, or as if you only get to be a *legitimate* person in time, by *choosing* a path and *doing* something. In which case children, for example, wouldn't really count. Women neither, perhaps, in theory, at least not on an equal footing. And the unemployed, the homeless, they wouldn't either.

The age in which we think we live. I always have this feeling: it's different than the one we think.

My body works constructing the images, bodies working like pistons. Hands working like pistons. Melting snow with traces of rust in old window frames is real. I arrive at a reading, only then to leave again, unable to bear being present. I leave early, like everyone else I feel like the only survivor in a plane crash. To be outside of something, the whole time, excluded.

WE AGREE ON a *casual* meeting, and your face tries to convince me our seeing each other is innocent, rather funny, in fact. When something is presented in that way, I think: it is neither. Not innocent, not funny. There is nothing innocent about concealing something from a person of whom one is fond. It's not about feeling, or the absence of feeling. Love, or the absence of love. It's about saying *I love you* in one room—and it being true. And the next minute, in another room, to another person, saying the same thing, quite as truthfully. *I love you.* Not to superimpose the two images, or declarations of love; not to see the image become blurred and nauseating, the way it does. Devoid. To be able to erect a wall down the middle of oneself, down the middle of one's language, so the two utterances are accorded their own chambers, there to rest unchallenged, by anything but absence. Parallel lives and nothing but open doors, possibilities.

What to be done with possibilities.

And this, recurring—I wouldn't want. I wouldn't want to hurt anyone.

No matter how much you narrow your eyes you will see a different reality than the one they see; the maddest of enterprises. And it has nothing to do with love or the absence of love. Children, removing goldfish from their bowls, dabbing them dry and putting them to bed under the sheets. The desire to see vistas, open land-scapes; fir trees felled, though bearing lofty nests with speckled eggs inside, close to the trunk, vertical meters of collapsing life.

A person can suffocate from not being able to see far, you tell me, though meaning: I want to see something *else*.

I'm not sure, but I think it was here that the thought first came to me. That those who leave us will be our judges in the end.

I DECIDED TO wheel my bike home, for once having the feeling that everything in the world was going too fast. The flagstones barely had time to lay themselves down beneath my feet. I remem-ber having to focus in order to believe they would be there for me. Sound, too, can have that kind of delay, I thought. Emotions, too, perhaps. A bit like thirst: you don't know you're thirsty until you start to drink.

Later, some months later, I'm sitting outside the same unlikely apartment buildings, on the same bathing jetty at Islands Brygge, wondering if I ever *was* in love with you. The first winter and the first summer. Whether I actually came to love you. I don't suppose I did. But always I had the feeling you could save me.

You probably still can, in a way. If I changed—if I became another instead of the tedium of more and more myself.

I may be sentimental, but I'm not half as nostalgic as you.

Even if you can no longer pick out the moments you live for, you can pick out those you live in spite of. That might be a comfort of sorts. At least, it's the way I try to look at it.

THEY WALK UP the uneven street. She tucks her arm under his. One of their numerous attempts that summer.

Because now it's different—because we're wiser now.

He indicates a café, she gives a shrug. She finds a table inside while he orders coffee.

I've been thinking about you and *objects*, he says. The way it makes you sad if you break something.

She looks up at him, thinking. Does it, she says after a pause. Her fingers have come to a halt. Maybe it does. I don't know, I suppose I've never felt it made sense whenever my parents said it's only an inanimate object. As if you weren't allowed to be sad. Prohibiting grief deemed to be irrational. What kind would be left, then. If we reject the grief that is out of proportion. Surely we can't distinguish like that. Isn't it all a matter of death.

Death, she repeats.

He thinks: you and your drama. And he loves her then. She can see that. He puts his hand on top of hers, her unsettled hand.

She can see the other woman like some strange fungus in his eyes.

She picks up his cup of coffee and blows into it a couple of times before drinking a sip. Maybe that's why he's unable to move on and love someone else. Because recollections always intrude. Every time he is on the verge of loving, truly loving her, or the other woman, he finds he can't.

Not forgetting or not loving, it's all the same to him.

It's the only way she can look at it; there are those who love, and those who do not. Those who can, and those who cannot. And then there is the tragic group, those who can love, but do not. Because they get confused, they mistake things. Forgetting something and choosing something.

He must make himself blind to imagine that he has now moved on, that he was able to forget; what kind of a person was it then he had to offer. Blind and deaf, and without a past.

The guilt of remembering something, remembering her, in the face of the new woman.

The guilt of being something *oneself.*

And now he is trying. He must not talk of it, but refrain from mentioning everything about which he thinks, her, about whom he thinks, and then everything will be all right. Albeit for the nausea of being so thoughtless; but then one will always have thoughts.

She sticks a hand in her pocket and rubs the key with her thumb, feeling for its teeth as the tongue feels for a sore in the mouth, passing tentatively across unfamiliar flesh.

I shouldn't drink coffee, he thinks. It's always the same whenever he drinks coffee; it makes me depressed.

You shouldn't drink coffee, she says casually.

You're right. I get so . . .

. . . troubled, she says.

Yes, he says. That's it: troubled.

SHE WAS IN her nightdress. She went down the stairs, in this long nightdress, it had peacocks on it, she tells him, at least I think they were peacocks. Or were they; yes, peacocks. Eight in all, if you counted all the way round. With tail feathers interlaced, shimmering colours, though dulled by age. I always thought those real peacocks, the ones in the pen at Toggerbo when we went for drives in the evening, or in the autumn when we went mushrooming there; that those peacocks were somehow wrong. That their colors were too strong. Too dark.

He nods. Perhaps thinking she ought not to reminisce all the time, spend so much energy remembering.

The consternation of remembering.

The consternation of not.

THE
LANDSCAPE

B UT THE SNOW. The way it keeps falling. My mother pulls a
tea bag out of the pot. She presses the last drops of liquid from
it, on the edge of her plate, then lifts it across the table with a hand
underneath to protect the tablecloth; her hand is a shadow on a
lawn, beneath a sky, faithfully following along over the landscape.
She nudges a piece of gingerbread cake to the side of her plate so it
doesn't get wet.

What is it you wanted to get done; what does the snow prevent
you from doing.

Blankets of snow, falling in different bands; how much wind,
how big the flakes. Overlapping belts of white.

A way of traversing a landscape.

A way of smothering the sound that exists; the sound of snow
falling.

Plans, and work postponed.

We have snuggled into blankets. Now it is she who frowns and
leans across the table. On the first day of the summer holidays she
plaited our hair into tight French braids so the salt water wouldn't
ruin it. Or so she didn't have to set it all the time; every time
an elastic slipped off a ponytail, whenever the water turned hair

into a slippery rope. With the tip of her index finger she turns a glass marble on the board, making the light reflect differently in its streaky color.

Is that mine.

Uh huh, I say. She picks it up and moves it in an arc over the board. A planet in its inevitable orbit. Then lowers it into a space there, as if to prove a point. Or to apologize.

She is a master of Chinese chequers; *there*, she says, looking up. First at me, then turning in her chair to look out at the road. There are no tracks in the snow there, not yet, there are no cars out. The sound of the snow as it falls, the non-sound made by *that*. Its thunder, and its absence.

Your turn, my mother says. She pours more tea, her eyes grow older. The voices of the snow are swallowed by the wind, at the bend by the lake.

Your turn, she repeats. I place a finger on a marble and follow a path across the board. No, not that one, another. Only the next comes to a dead end after four hops. In the minutes of my turn, only falling snow is heard. A sentence that may join all the world together, a way of walking that connects two places.

Are you sure about that, she asks me. I understand there must be a better move.

Yes, I say.

She puts down her cup, draws a green marble all the way through the board into my area. I love you, I think to myself.

I ASK IF we can eat in the kitchen. The darknesss is too oppressive here. My face is warm with sleep that never became sleep. A long day. An exhaustion that comes of the day. My father arriving home, his footsteps through the living room, to the piano. I hear him put down his car keys, see them reflect for a moment in the black varnished wood.

And then they are still and silent in their place. The lake gapes beneath the ice, but the winter is a lid on top of all that is living, all that is dead: as the snow that falls, all the living and all the dead.

Do you remember, I say quietly, when we found that big fish in the lake.

My mother looks up. She is standing with a teaspoon in her hand, removing pips from a cucumber, scraping one half, then the other. She has a steady hand. The same with fish, the way she removes the bones in a single movement, with ease.

I think so, she says. Last winter, was it. Or the one before. It must have been the one before.

It was trapped in the ice, I say. And my hands have come to a halt; my eyes notice them, the way they have come to rest on the chopping board.

I am not breathing.

We both know it must be the winter before last, because last winter we couldn't see each other. I had *made a choice*, she said. After that she fell ill, then presumably forgot her disappointment; color washes from wood if only it is left long enough in the sea. It doesn't disappear, but becomes like the winter: only lighter. Increasingly iridescent, a price on my head that continues to rise. A competition in which we have forgotten to time ourselves.

It must have been, I say. Last year. Why hasn't he said hello, I ask.

She raises her eyebrows and looks so sad all of a sudden.

Perhaps he's, I don't know . . .

She turns the cucumbers on the chopping board, slices them into staves, dices them, then lifts the board over to a bowl of yogurt, sweeping it clean with the spine of the blade.

Tired, I suggest.

Tired, yes. That'll be it.

I crush three cloves of garlic and peel them, passing them on to her with the garlic press. I put the dry skins in the trash. Hi, Dad, I call into the living room. He has sat down at the piano. It needs tuning, always some note that resists. He plays as if there's something important he wishes to announce to someone.

What is it about that fish.

I don't know why. I just started thinking about it.

It did look so very strange. Caught in the ice, and frozen solid.

I nod. It's funny, but it suddenly feels like—well, a long time ago.

It is, she says. Rinsing the chopping board and wiping it dry. I suppose he must be, tired.

He gives me a kiss on the cheek. Do you want red wine, he asks. Yes, I say to please him. Or to comfort myself. That's probably it. I drink three glasses while we eat. They open another bottle. Should we open another bottle. Yes, why not.

What are you doing, she asks me as we brush our teeth before bed. That won't help. I shrug. I shouldn't have come.

Of course you should. The way you're feeling.

I shrug again. I think there's something fine about repeating it all the time.

BE CAREFUL WITH that dish. It means a lot to me.

I will.

Thanks, she says. Do you think you'll be coming home more often now.

Yes, I lie.

She smiles. Puts the dishes in the dishwasher. Straightens up and holds on to the counter for support. That's good, she says. You're always welcome, you know that.

I nod. This is the way things are right now. But who of us is welcome. That's the feeling I'm left with. I'm someone else. She doesn't know who it is she's inviting. She knows who it is she misses. In a way we are the same. I, too, miss something that no longer exists. I am careful with the dish and put a napkin down on it before placing the smaller dish on top. I tear open the wrapping of some tomatoes and put them in a bowl. The things you forget have to be just as real as those you remember. If not more so. That hasn't altered. Does a head scarf look silly, I ask her. Is it too Suzanne Brøgger.

No, I don't think so. It looks good. Color suits you.

Did she say I was always welcome.

There is a sense of repetition that becomes impossible—a thought that there are no rules as such. That there is a place in the world for one sorrow, and a place in the world for another. That all the time, we discover new people to miss.

There. I turn toward her, holding a red scarf to my head. It'll look good on you, she says.

I look at myself in the windows, the mirrors of their glass in the evening. The steam now gone.

YOU'RE NOT SLEEPING.

No, I'm not sleeping. My mother sits down on the sofa opposite. She gets up again almost in the same movement, places a log in the wood stove. Opens the inlet. The influx of air sucks flames from the embers.

She sits down again and draws a throw over her. It's impossible to tell what she wants. I am lying on the made-up sofa, the rear cushions heaped in a pile at the end.

I don't know why you won't sleep upstairs. The bed's made up and the heat's on.

The fire, I say. It's nice to lie here and look at the fire.

She nods, watching it with me, staring into the flames. We both think of my grandmother, the time she lay here, the last winter she was alive. I know exactly that it is what my mother is thinking about. The way her own mother was unable to reconcile herself with the glass window of the stove, the way she kept calling for us to tell us this: the house is on fire.

There's *meant* to be fire, we said, it's a stove for heating. It stays inside, nothing will happen.

Why didn't we just move her into the office, I ask out of the blue.

My mother shrugs. That's where I get it from, I think to myself. My shoulders are an echo of my mother's.

She was afraid in the night, I think. How could we let her lie like that, I ask into the room. Afraid in the night.

She slept eventually, my mother says, defensively.

Perhaps, I say. Or maybe her face grew tired. My fingers feel my own face, as though to see for themselves. Was it tired of looking sad. Was there any clarification. There was no way of telling.

Who is it you're grieving over anyway, she suddenly asks.

I am not even surprised by her question.

I don't know, I say calmly. Have you noticed the apple tree, I ask.

The fire settles. The wind has died, it calms the flame.

Which one, she asks. She draws a cushion under her head and makes herself comfortable.

I can't help thinking about her body underneath the blanket. Like the plaster cast of a body.

Mine, I say quietly.

Have you got your *own* apple tree, she asks. Which one is it.

Don't you remember, that afternoon. We were each given a tree. It was your idea. I chose first, I don't even think the others were that interested. I don't think they cared.

Oh, says my mother. I do remember now, faintly. The low tree, the one you can see from the bedroom.

Yes, that's the one, I nod.

My mother's legs, her blue chest. You can see the movements of her heart inside her chest.

I'm not sure I know who you're grieving over.

No, I say. How could you, when I don't even know myself. Have you noticed the tree, it's still got apples on it.

Has it. That's good for the birds.

What sort are they. They're red. And very dark. Not Ingrid Marie, I'd recognize those.

Is it Jakob, or the new one, she asks.

I turn onto my back and look through the room. The joists slice it apart. When can you take sprigs in, I ask. Will they blossom if you take them in now.

I don't think so. They need buds first. In March you should be able to. Then they'll flower. She talks about the spring, March, April, May. I'm not listening. I'm already asleep.

Josefine Klougart has been hailed as one of Denmark's greatest contemporary writers. She is the first Danish author ever to have two of her first three books nominated for the Nordic Council Literature Prize, and has been compared to Joan Didion, Anne Carson, and Virginia Woolf.

Martin Aitken has translated dozens of books from the Danish, including works by Dorthe Nors, Jussi Adler-Olsen, Peter Høeg, and Kim Leine.

**OPEN
LETTER**

WWW.OPENLETTERBOOKS.ORG

**OPEN
LETTER**

WWW.OPENLETTERBOOKS.ORG